ABOUT THE AUTHOR

Barbara Cartland, the world's most famous romantic novelist, who is also an historian, playwright, lecturer, political speaker and television personality, has now written over 632 books and sold over 600 million copies all over the world.

She has also had many historical works published and has written four autobiographies as well as the biographies of her mother and that of her brother, Ronald Cartland, who was the first Member of Parliament to be killed in the last war. This book has a preface by Sir Winston Churchill and has just been published with an introduction by the late Sir Arthur Bryant.

"Love at the Helm" a novel written with the help and inspiration of the late Earl Mountbatten of Burma, Great Uncle of His Royal Highness The Prince of Wales, is being sold for the Mountbatten Memorial Trust.

She has broken the world record for the last seventeen years by writing an average of twenty-three books a year. In the Guinness Book of Records she is listed as the world's top-selling author.

In 1978 she sang an Album of Love Songs with the Royal Philharmonic Orchestra.

In private life Barbara Cartland, who is a Dame of Grace of the Order of St. John of Jerusalem, Chairman of the St. John Council in Hertfordshire and Deputy President of the St. John Ambulance Brigade, has fought for better conditions and salaries for Midwives and Nurses.

She championed the cause for the Elderly in 1956 invoking a Government Enquiry into the "Housing Conditions of Old People".

In 1962 she had the Law of England changed so that Local Authorities had to provide camps for their own Gypsies. This has meant that since then thousands and thousands of Gypsy children have been able to go to School which they had never been able to do in the past, as their caravans were moved every twenty-four hours by the Police.

There are now fourteen camps in Hertfordshire and Barbara Cartland has her own Romany Gypsy Camp called Barbaraville by the Gypsies.

Her designs "Decorating with Love" are being sold all over the USA and the National Home Fashions League made her in 1981, "Woman of Achievement".

Barbara Cartland's book "Getting Older, Growing Younger" has been published in Great Britain and the USA and her fifth Cookery Book, "The Romance of Food" is now being used by the House of Commons.

In 1984 she received at Kennedy Airport, America's Bishop Wright Air Industry Award for her contribution to the development of aviation. In 1931 she and two RAF Officers thought of, and carried the first aeroplane-towed glider airmail.

During the War she was Chief Lady Welfare Officer in Bedfordshire looking after 20,000 Service men and women. She thought of having a pool of Wedding Dresses at the War Office so a service Bride could hire a gown for the day.

She bought 1,000 secondhand gowns without coupons for the ATS, the WAAFS and the WRENS. In 1945 Barbara Cartland received the Certificate of Merit from Eastern Command.

In 1964 Barbara Cartland founded the National Association for Health of which she is the President, as a front for all the Health Stores and for any product made as alternative medicine.

This has now a £500,000,000 turnover a year, with one third going in export.

In January 1988 she received "La Medaille de Vermeil de la Ville de Paris", (The Gold Medal of Paris). This is the highest award to be given by the City of Paris for ACHIEVEMENT – 25 million books sold in France.

In March 1988 Barbara Cartland was asked by the Indian Government to open their Health Resort outside Delhi. This is almost the largest Health Resort in the world.

Barbara Cartland was received with great enthusiasm by her fans, who also fêted her at a Reception in the City and she received the gift of an embossed plate from the Government.

Barbara Cartland was made a Dame of the Order of the British Empire in the 1991 New Year's Honours List, by Her Majesty The Queen for her contribution to literature and for her work for the Community.

AWARDS

1945   Received Certificate of Merit, Eastern
        Command.

1953   Made a Commander of the Order of
        St. John of Jerusalem. Invested by
        H.R.H. The Duke of Gloucester at
        Buckingham Palace.

1972   Invested as Dame of Grace of the
        Order of St. John in London by The
        Lord Prior, Lord Cacia.

1981   Receives "Achiever of the Year" from
        the National Home Furnishing
        Association in Colorado Springs,
        U.S.A.

1984   Receives Bishop Wright Air Industry
        Award at Kennedy Airport, for
        inventing the aeroplane-towed Glider.

1988   Receives from Monsieur Chirac, The
        Prime Minister, the Gold Medal of
        the City of Paris, at the Hôtel de la
        Ville, Paris, for selling 25 million
        books and giving a lot of employment.

1991   Invested as Dame of the Order of The
        British Empire, by H.M. The Queen
        at Buckingham Palace, for her
        contribution to literature.

*Also by Barbara Cartland and
available from Mandarin Paperbacks*

THE LOVE LIGHT OF APOLLO

Her Majesty Queen Victoria anxious to separate H.R.H. Princess Marigold from Prince Holden insists she must attend the Funeral of H.R.H. Prince Eumenus of Malia which is to take place in Athens.

Furious at being sent away from the man she loves, Princess Marigold persuades Avila Grandell, who is almost her double, to take her place.

Avila, the daughter of a Country Vicar whose Mother is Greek, can speak the language, but has never been to Greece, which is something she longs to do.

Her Mother is doubtful, but Avila pleads to be allowed to take Princess Marigold's place as the representative of the Queen at the Funeral.

Convinced by Prince Holden that their plan is foolproof, Mrs Grandell finally agrees.

How Princess Marigold and Prince Holden marry in secret.

How Avila thinks the voyage will be an adventure and finds it is even more exciting.

How she leaves Athens in tears but how she finds the 'Light of Apollo' again, is all told in this ingenious and romantic story, the 510th book by Barbara Cartland.

BARBARA CARTLAND

The Love Light of Apollo

Miss Fredda J. Corbett
1176 King Richard
Las Vegas, NV 89119

Mandarin

A Mandarin Paperback

THE LOVE LIGHT OF APOLLO

First published in Great Britain 1996
by Mandarin Paperbacks
an imprint of Reed International Books Ltd
Michelin House, 81 Fulham Road, London SW3 6RB
and Auckland, Melbourne, Singapore and Toronto

Copyright © Cartland Promotions 1996

The author has asserted her moral rights

A CIP catalogue record for this title
is available from the British Library
ISBN 0 7493 1273 4

Phototypeset by Intype London Ltd
Printed and bound in Great Britain
by Cox & Wyman Ltd, Reading, Berks.

AUTHOR'S NOTE

I fell in love with Greece when I first read "The Splendour of Greece" by Robert Payne.

When I went there I found this fascinating book answered so many questions and made me understand the mystery and beauty of the gods.

Delos where Apollo was born is just as I have described it.

Some of the Greek families are just a part of my story but the description of the Parthenon in the Erechtheion is exactly as I saw and felt it.

After 2,500 years Greece is still a mystical enigma to the Western World.

Just as Robert Payne puts it so clearly.

"The splendour of Greece still lights our skies, reaching over America and Asia and lands which the Greeks never dream existed. There would be no Christianity as we know it without the fertilizing influence of the Greek Fathers of the Church, who owed their training to Greek philosophy.

By a strange accident all the images of Buddha in the Far East can be traced back to portraits of Alexander, who seemed to the Greeks to be Apollo incarnate. We owe to the Greeks the beginning of science and the beginning of thought.

They built the loveliest temples ever made, carved marble with delicacy and strength, and set in motion the questing mind which refuses to believe there are any bounds to reason.

That is why we journey to Greece like pilgrims to a feast."

CHAPTER ONE
1874

"No! No! No! I will not do it – I will not!"

Princess Marigold's voice rose to a shriek on the last word.

Pulling off her slipper she flung it at her Comptroller, Colonel Bassett.

As this had happened to him before, he swiftly side-stepped.

The slipper landed on top of a cabinet, knocking over a pretty piece of Dresden china.

Princess Marigold was lying on the sofa and now she said in a slightly quieter voice:

"You can inform Her Majesty that I will not go to Greece, and that is the end of the matter!"

Colonel Bassett sighed.

"I am afraid, Your Royal Highness, that you cannot refuse a Royal Command."

"Why not?" Princess Marigold asked sharply. "This is supposed to be a free country."

Colonel Bassett did not reply, and after a moment she said furiously:

"Free! Of course it is free for everyone, except someone like myself who is supposed to be Royal, but without a throne, and without anyone paying any attention to what I want, or do not want to do!"

This again was something Colonel Bassett had heard before, and he remained silent.

Then unexpectedly the door opened and a voice said:

"Is anyone at home?"

The Princess sat up abruptly.

"Holden!" she exclaimed. "Thank goodness you have come! What do you think has happened?"

Prince Holden came further into the room, nodded to Colonel Bassett and walked towards the Princess.

He was a tall, broad-shouldered, handsome young man with somewhat Germanic features.

"I heard you shouting," the Prince said, "so I knew there was trouble."

"Trouble!" Princess Marigold echoed. "Oh, Holden, Holden, what am I to do?"

The Prince took the Princess's hand and raised it to his lips.

"You are upsetting yourself," he said, "but you promised me that I should cope with your troubles and you would not become agitated over them."

"Agitated?" Princess Marigold exclaimed. "Of course I am agitated! Have you heard what that monstrous old woman here in Windsor Castle wants me to do?"

Prince Holden turned his head towards Colonel Bassett.

"What has happened?" he asked.

"Her Majesty," Colonel Bassett answered, speaking in a somewhat pompous voice, "has informed Her Royal Highness that she is to represent Great Britain at the Funeral of His Royal Highness Prince Eumenus of Malia."

"Oh, is he dead?" Prince Holden replied. "I heard he was ill."

"His Royal Highness is dead, and his body has been embalmed so that he can be buried in Athens, in two weeks' time," the Colonel said. "While he was not of any great diplomatic importance Her Majesty feels that she personally, and of course Great Britain, should be represented at the ceremony."

Prince Holden had been listening attentively.

Now he said quietly as he turned towards the Princess:

"You will have to go, my Dearest."

"And leave you?" Princess Marigold exclaimed. "Can you not see what Queen Victoria is up to? She had never approved of our engagement, and now she is doing everything in her power to separate us!"

"She will never do that," Prince Holden said.

At the same time there was an anxious expression in his eyes.

After months of discussion, Queen Victoria had finally allowed Princess Marigold, who was a near relation, to become engaged to Prince Holden of Allenberg.

No one could pretend that it was a marriage of prestige for the Princess.

But she had fallen madly in love with Prince Holden, and she firmly refused to consider any other man who was suggested to her.

Ever since she had been small, Princess Marigold had been what Queen Victoria thought of as a problem.

She had come to England with her Father and Mother after Prince Dimitri had been thrown out of Panaeros.

It was a Greek island where his family had reigned for generations.

Queen Victoria had found the family a burden on her hands.

At first Prince Dimitri had begged Her Majesty over and over again to send British ships and British guns to get him back his throne.

When she refused to do so and he died, his wife Helen, who was English, and a cousin of the Queen, had died of a broken heart.

In fact, she had never forgiven Queen Victoria for refusing her husband's request.

It was whispered amongst the Courtiers that she had put a Greek curse on the Queen before she herself died.

Whether this was true or not, she had certainly left Her Majesty a bundle of trouble in the shape of her only child.

The Princess had been christened Mary Gloriana Amethyst Victoria.

The names had been chosen as compliments to her grandparents, her Godmothers, and of course the Queen of Great Britain.

As soon as she could talk, Princess Mary, as it had been decided she should be called, refused to answer to any name, except that of Marigold.

No one quite understood why it had taken her fancy.

Yet she insisted over and over again to her

Nurses, her Governesses, and anyone else who would listen, that her name was Marigold.

It became impossible to call by her real name a child who would not answer to anything but the name she had chosen.

First her Nurses gave in to her whim, then her Governesses and Tutors.

Finally, through sheer exasperation, Queen Victoria herself.

Princess Marigold she then became, and was undoubtedly a 'thorn in the flesh' of her benefactress.

She was brought up at Windsor Castle.

There was plenty of room in that huge, unwieldy edifice for a dozen children, if necessary.

But it was often felt by those in attendance that it was too small for Princess Marigold.

She was invariably in trouble of one sort or another.

However as she grew up she became extremely pretty.

She resembled her Mother with her fair hair and pink-and-white English complexion.

But her eyes were definitely Greek, dark, expressive and very beautiful.

The combination was so striking that whoever saw her looked, then looked again.

This made Queen Victoria determined to marry off Princess Marigold as soon as possible.

It would certainly mean a quieter and less turbulent atmosphere inside the Castle.

Her Majesty might have known, however, that anyone she chose for her troublesome relative would be unacceptable.

Usually before Princess Marigold had even seen the man in question she decided that she would not marry him.

Crown Princes were suggested one after another.

All of whom were, as Queen Victoria knew, only too eager to be more closely associated with Britain and her ever-growing Empire.

Princess Marigold said "No! No! No!"

Princes were invited to England.

They came cocky and pleased with themselves, confident they would go home closely united through marriage to the British throne.

They left with 'their tails between their legs'.

A sharp little voice now said: "No! No! No!" to everything they suggested!

Then, quite unexpectedly, with no scheming by Queen Victoria, in fact it was without her knowledge, Princess Marigold met Prince Holden of Allenberg.

He had come to England to stay with friends.

His visit had not been notified as a Royal Occasion to Buckingham Palace nor to Windsor Castle.

It was just by chance that Princess Marigold, having nothing to do one afternoon, thought she would go to Ranelagh and watch the Polo.

She had been invited many times, but generally found it rather boring.

However when she looked in her diary she found there was nothing special for her that day.

She decided on an impulse she would drive to Ranelagh.

A good-looking young Duke with whom she

had danced the previous night had told her he was playing against a team arranged by the German Embassy.

"I believe they rather fancy themselves," he had said, "but I am quite certain, Your Royal Highness, we will win. We are in tip-top form and have won every game we have played so far this Season."

He had paused, then added:

"We would of course be very honoured if you would come to watch us tomorrow."

Princess Marigold had enjoyed herself that evening.

No one had pestered her to go home early, or told her that she could not dance for the third time with the same partner.

She had therefore given orders when she woke that she would go to Ranelagh.

This meant that she had to take a Lady-in Waiting with her.

The one whose turn it was complained bitterly:

"I have a headache!" she told the other Lady-in-Waiting. "Why can not that tiresome girl stay here instead of gallivanting off to watch Polo where I will doubtless have to sit in the sun."

She gave a sigh and then went on:

"I shall then have to listen to her saying all the way home that she was bored!"

It must have been a surprise later that Princess Marigold was in such a good temper.

Especially as when they finally drove back to Windsor Castle it was quite late in the evening.

"I must see you tomorrow," Prince Holden had said as he helped her into the carriage.

"You will not forget?" the Princess had replied in a soft voice.

"How could you imagine I could forget anything that concerns you?" he asked.

They had looked into each other's eyes.

It was with the greatest reluctance that the Prince moved away so that the footman could shut the door of the carriage.

As Princess Marigold drove off she bent forward to wave to him.

He stood watching until the carriage was out of sight.

Prince Holden had come to Windsor Castle the next day to pay his humble respects to Queen Victoria.

She had received him without much enthusiasm.

Allenberg was a very small South German Principality and of no particular importance.

However Her Majesty was determined to prevent the unscrupulous manner in which the Russians were trying to exert influence in a number of the Balkan States.

They had already infiltrated into Servia and other North Balkan States.

The Tsar of Russia had fortunately not been successful in gaining control of Bulgaria.

Prince Alexander of Battenberg had refused to act as a Russian 'puppet'.

Finally the Russians kidnapped the Prince and forced him to abdicate at pistol-point.

Queen Victoria had been furious.

"Russia behaves and has behaved shamefully!" she raged.

It was because of what had happened in Bulgaria that finally she became more amenable to the idea of Princess Marigold marrying Prince Holden.

However, Bulgaria was a large country, while Allenberg was a very small one.

Over and over again she told Princess Marigold how advantageous it would be for her to marry a man who could make her a Queen.

To Queen Victoria's surprise however, for almost the first time since the death of the Prince Consort, she found she could not have her own way.

"I intend, Cousin Victoria," Princess Marigold said firmly, "to marry Prince Holden, even if I have to elope with him and am never allowed to set foot on English soil again!"

Finally, reluctantly, because nothing she could say would move Princess Marigold, Queen Victoria conceded.

The engagement between Prince Holden of Allenberg and the Princess was to be announced the following week.

Unfortunately, the day before the engagement should have appeared in the newspapers, an elderly relative of the Queen and the Princess died.

This meant they were in black for six months.

There was no question of even a minor Royal Wedding taking place until the time of mourning was past.

The Queen therefore decided that their engagement was to be kept secret from everyone except those living in Windsor Castle.

The public announcement would be made when the actual date of the wedding was decided.

Now in a voice that was almost hysterical Princess Marigold said:

"Do you not understand, Holden, that Her Majesty will use the death of Prince Eumenus as an excuse to keep us in mourning."

She paused a moment before continuing:

"She is hoping and praying that we will become bored with waiting and then she can marry me off to some doddering old King whose throne is crumbling under him!"

Prince Holden put his hand over the Princess's.

"We have a little more than two months to go," he said, "and I cannot believe that Prince Eumenus who was of little importance, could expect us to mourn for longer than that."

"But I will not leave you and go to Greece," Princess Marigold retorted. "I know exactly how Her Majesty's mind works! She is thinking that because Papa was Greek, I might find someone there of more importance than you."

Prince Holden was aware this was true.

But as there was nothing he could say, he raised the Princess's hand to his lips.

"Also," the Princess went on, "you promised that you would take me away in your yacht. I have not yet told the Queen, but I have decided whom we would take with us as a chaperon – old Lady Milne."

She smiled at him and then went on:

"If we give her enough to drink she will sleep all through the afternoon and evening, and not interfere with us at all."

"No one shall ever do that," the Prince said firmly.

"But that is exactly what the Queen is trying to do!" the Princess said.

Now the anger was back in her voice.

"Surely there is someone else who could go?" Prince Holden said turning to Colonel Bassett.

He was still standing somewhat uncomfortably by the door.

He was used to Princess Marigold's tantrums.

Yet he could never make up his mind whether it was best to leave the room, without permission or to stay.

If he did the latter he had to listen to her raging at him or anyone else.

"Even if there were Your Royal Highness," he said in answer to the Prince, "I doubt if Her Majesty would change her mind and send someone else in place of Her Royal Highness."

"Nevertheless, you had better find someone!" Princess Marigold said sharply. "For I am not going, even if I have to stay in bed and say I am too ill to travel."

"I want you to be with me," Prince Holden said in a low, caressing tone. "I was so looking forward to taking you across the North Sea to Denmark or anywhere else you preferred."

"And I want to be with .. you," the Princess said.

She was looking up into his eyes.

For a moment they forgot that Colonel Bassett was in the room.

"I want to stand on deck at night and look at

the stars," the Princess said, "and I want to keep counting the days until we can be married."

"That is what I am doing," the Prince said, and his fingers tightened on hers.

"Then let us defy the Queen," Princess Marigold said, "and send someone else in my place! As long as there is someone in dismal black with a Union Jack hanging over their heads, no one will care whether I am there or not."

"I agree," the Prince said, "but I doubt if anyone would be brave enough to impersonate you and risk the wrath of Her Majesty."

"There must be someone if we could only find her," Princess Marigold persisted. "Surely you know someone, Colonel Bassett?"

"I am afraid not, Your Royal Highness!" the Colonel answered quickly.

"Oh, how can you be so unhelpful?" the Princess said. "I thought you were on my side!"

"Your Highness is well aware," the Colonel said, "that if I encouraged you to intrigue against Her Majesty's orders, I would be dismissed instantly, if I were not taken to the Tower of London as a traitor!"

He spoke lightly.

At the same time, both the Prince and Princess knew there was a great deal of truth in what he said.

As if he thought it was a mistake to continue the conversation, Colonel Bassett said:

"If Your Royal Highness will excuse me, I have a great many letters that need my attention."

"Yes, yes, of course," the Princess replied.

The words had hardly left her lips before

Colonel Bassett had hurried from the room, shutting the door behind him.

The Prince put his arms round the Princess and pulled her close against him.

"I love you," he said, "and it is an agony to think you have to go away from me! I suppose I could make the excuse that I too wish to attend Prince Eumenus's Funeral."

"The Queen will not believe that," the Princess said, "because the other night, when she mentioned to you he was ill, you said quite positively that you had never ever heard of him."

The Prince sighed.

"I remember that now, and I cannot think why I did not keep my mouth shut!"

"It is the sort of thing Her Majesty would remember," Princess Marigold said. "Anyway, I am sure she would not allow you to travel with me – I suppose in a Battleship, unless they are being measly and sending me by train."

"If you are representing Her Majesty, then you will go by sea," the Prince said.

Being of German origin he was extremely knowledgeable on protocol.

The Princess was sure he was right.

"But I want to be with you, darling Holden!" she said. "In your yacht, and away from everyone including all these ghastly old fuddy-duddies, who keep saying I should not marry you!"

"I am terrified in case you ever agree with them," the Prince said.

"You know I would never, never do that!" the Princess answered. "I love you, Holden, and I had never loved anyone until I met you."

He pulled her into his arms and kissed her passionately, until they were both breathless.

If the Queen had known that the Princess received Prince Holden without being chaperoned by a Lady-in-Waiting, she would have been outraged.

They were both aware that it was lucky that Prince Holden had come to find her when she was with her Comptroller.

It was Colonel Bassett who had suggested that it would be best for him to see the Princess alone in the mornings.

Otherwise she would have her two aged and very garrulous Ladies-in-Waiting with her.

Now they could discuss privately plans on which they had not yet made a final decision without it being talked about all over the Palace.

It had therefore been a golden opportunity for the Prince to be alone with Princess Marigold.

This was something with difficulty, they were continually trying to find in the Castle.

Because the Queen disapproved of the engagement, she deliberately put every obstacle in their way.

Now as the Prince raised his head, he said in a voice that was slightly unsteady:

"I love you, my Dearest! I love you, and I know that once we are married, we will be very happy. But I find this waiting intolerable."

"So do I," the Princess said, "and it will be worse still when I have to go away. I suppose it will take a fortnight, or even three weeks to go to Greece, attend the Funeral, make myself agreeable to a whole collection of boring people and then come slowly home."

She gave an exclamation of anger as she said:

"I am sure that ghastly old woman will tell the ship's Captain to move at one knot per hour, just so that I cannot be with you!"

"You are not to upset yourself, darling," the Prince said. "I swear we will be married the very day the six months of mourning ends!"

"If she will let us!" the Princess said.

She gave a sudden cry.

"Suppose . . suppose, Holden, while I am away, she somehow gets rid of you? I would not trust her not to have you kidnapped, or sent to Outer Mongolia, or some such place!"

Prince Holden laughed.

"Now you are just imagining things," he said. "I promise I will keep very quiet and out of sight, so as not to annoy Her Majesty, until you return."

"I will not go! I swear I will not go!" Princess Marigold cried. "There must be someone who can go in my place! Think, Holden, think! Who do we know who looks like me?"

As this was something they had not thought of before, the Prince stared at her.

Then he said:

"It is rather funny that you should say that! I saw a girl last week who was in fact, very like you."

"Was she a relative of mine?" Princess Marigold asked.

"I was staying with the Duke of Ilchester," the Prince went on, "and I went to Church on Sunday because the Duchess asked me rather pointedly, I thought, to escort her."

"Yes, yes, go on!" the Princess urged.

"It was a pleasant village Service. But I was surprised to see in the Church in the front pew, sitting beside an attractive Lady a girl who might actually have been your sister."

"I do not believe it!" Princess Marigold exclaimed. "Who is she?"

"I asked the Duchess afterwards, and she said that the Lady was the Vicar's wife, and she was Greek."

"Greek?" the Princess exclaimed. "And the girl who looked like me?"

"Her daughter, named Avila, I was informed," the Prince said. "I meant to tell you about it, but I forgot until just now."

He smiled before he added:

"How can I think of anyone, except you?"

"If she looks like me," Princess Marigold said, "and if she has some Greek blood in her, then let us offer to pay her, although of course we can put it politely as a gift, to go to Greece in my place."

The Prince laughed.

"Now you are Fairy-Tale-ing again! I cannot believe for a moment she would be allowed to go, or that she could take your place without anyone being aware of it."

"If she takes my place just before I am supposed to step aboard the ship, draped of course in black, her face obscured by a crêpe veil, who is to know?"

"Are you really serious?" Prince Holden asked. "You must be aware that the whole idea is crazy! The Queen would be absolutely furious if she learns of it."

"*If* she learns of it!" the Princess emphasised. "Now, Holden, we have to be clever about this. I know how brilliant you are at organisation. Surely you can organise this for me?"

She paused for a moment before she went on firmly: "I love you! I love you! To be away from you even for a day is agony. To be gone from you for weeks I think would kill me!"

"My Darling, my sweet, how can you say such things?" the Prince asked.

He pulled her close to him.

He would have kissed her again, but the Princess put her fingers over his lips.

"Promise me," she begged, "that you will try to make it possible for me to come with you in your yacht! Promise!"

The Prince looked down at her and was lost.

Finally he said:

"I promise, but . . ."

Whatever he would have said was lost as Princess Marigold was kissing him wildly.

CHAPTER TWO

Driving his Chaise with Princess Marigold beside him, Prince Holden said:

"We have escaped for the moment, and it was just luck that I sat next to the Duchess of Ilchester at dinner last night."

"I think Fate is on our side," the Princess replied, "and now we have to persuade this Greek woman that it is advantageous for her daughter to go to Athens in my place."

The Prince looked serious.

He was thinking privately that it was very unlikely the Vicar's wife would agree to anything so extraordinary.

What was more, he was quite certain their plot would be discovered and Queen Victoria would be furious with them both.

However he knew better than to say so at this moment.

As they drove on Princess Marigold said:

"It will be so wonderful to get away from everything in your yacht. You will have to plan it all out very carefully so that I leave at the same time as the girl goes to Athens."

Because he was enjoying being alone with the

Princess, Prince Holden did not argue about it and made no reply.

He had very cleverly arranged that the Lady-in-Waiting should travel in another Chaise behind them.

"I am sorry," he said, "but there really is not enough room for three people in the front of this Chaise, and I cannot imagine that anyone would want to sit behind us with the groom."

Because they had left Windsor Castle early in the morning, there were no Senior Officials about.

They had driven off as the Prince had arranged.

The Lady-in-Waiting, Lady Bedstone, came behind.

The Princess had chosen her carefully because she was old, slightly deaf and delighted to be going to luncheon with the Duke and Duchess of Ilchester.

"I told the Duchess," the Prince said when he was explaining to the Princess what he had arranged, "that you were longing to see her garden, which I had told you was very beautiful, and you also wished to meet and have a talk with the Vicar's wife, if that was possible."

"Was she surprised?" Princess Marigold enquired.

"She was, until I explained that no one in the Castle was Greek, and the few who spoke the language did so, in your opinion, very badly."

"If everything goes the way you have planned it, it will be wonderful!" the Princess said.

She had no idea that Prince Holden had lain awake all night wondering how he could persuade her to change her mind.

He finally decided that he would rely on the Vicar's wife.

He was sure she would refuse to allow her daughter to take part in a lie by pretending to be the Princess.

Princess Marigold was thrilled however at the way everything was going.

She put her hand on the Prince's knee as she said:

"I love you, Holden, and I swear that nothing and nobody shall stop us from being married the very day I am out of mourning!"

"If all else fails," the Prince said blithely, "we will run away. We can be married in France, or anywhere else we go. Then Her Majesty, however important she may be, can do nothing about it."

"I expect she will think up some terrible punishment!" Princess Marigold said. "But she will not be able to prevent me from becoming your wife.'

"No one can prevent that!" the Prince asserted.

He was, like Princess Marigold, head-over-heels in love.

He realised of course that it would also be of tremendous benefit to his Principality to be allied to the British throne.

He had been attracted by a number of women in the past, and they by him.

He had however, never felt as he felt now.

At the same time he was aware that he must keep his head.

He was trying to prevent Princess Marigold from doing something which would incur the wrath of Queen Victoria.

He was well aware that everyone was frightened of Her Majesty including the Prince of Wales.

He had thought at his first interview that she was the most awe-inspiring person he had ever met in the whole of his life.

He knew his Father would be extremely annoyed if the Queen turned her back on him.

It would be a catastrophe if he and the Princess were not accepted at Windsor Castle in the future.

But the sun was shining and Princess Marigold loved him!

It seemed impossible that the future could be dull and dismal for them both.

They reached the Duke's house, which was only about six miles from the Castle.

He owned a number of other houses, but Chester Park was one of the most impressive.

Set in five-thousand acres of land, it had been in the family for centuries.

It had been added to by a number of different generations.

As they drove up the drive, Prince Holden thought it was more of a Palace than a countryhouse.

The Duchess greeted Princess Marigold affectionately, exclaiming as they entered the Drawing-Room:

"It is delightful to see Your Royal Highness and such a surprise!"

"I know your garden is beautiful," the Princess replied, "and as I had nothing dull and formal to do today, it was a perfect opportunity to come here with Holden."

The Prince bowed and kissed the Duchess's hand.

When the Duke joined them they went in to luncheon.

Half-way through the meal the Duchess said:

"Prince Holden tells me you want to speak with Mrs. Grandell, who is Greek."

"I would love to do so, if it is not too much trouble," Princess Marigold replied. "I am so frightened that now that Papa and Mama are dead I shall forget my Greek, and have to learn it from a book, which is never the same as speaking the language."

"I am sure that is true," the Duchess agreed, "and I sent a message to Mrs. Grandell telling her that you, Ma'am, would call at about three o'clock."

"That is kind of you," the Princess said. "Do tell me, where does she come from in Greece?"

It seemed to her that the Duchess was suddenly at a loss for words.

She looked across the table at her husband who said quickly:

"Mrs. Grandell is a very reserved woman and seldom talks to anyone about Greece or the time when she left there."

The Duke then went on to discuss with the Prince some horses he had just bought.

The conversation about Mrs. Grandell thus came to an abrupt end.

Princess Marigold, who was very quick-witted, guessed there was some secret.

It was something she was not meant to find out, and she wondered what it could possibly be.

She managed however, to seem extremely interested in the garden which she was shown after luncheon.

But she was really counting the minutes until they could leave.

As they drove down the drive with Lady Bedstone, the Lady-in-Waiting following them, the Princess heaved a sigh of relief.

"I have never known time pass so slowly!" she complained.

"You must not be disappointed, my Darling," the Prince said, "if Mrs. Grandell will not agree to what you suggest, and we have to find somebody else."

"I cannot imagine there are many other people in the world who look exactly like me!" the Princess replied.

"Perhaps I was mistaken," Prince Holden said a little uncomfortably. "After all, I only saw a girl in Church."

"We will soon know whether you were right or wrong," the Prince said as he drew up his Chaise at the Vicarage.

The Princess had been sensible enough to tell Lady Bedstone that it would be a mistake for her to come into the Vicarage with them.

"The Duchess said," she told her when they were alone for a moment, "that Mrs. Grandell is very reserved. I am sure therefore, you will understand when I ask you to wait outside."

"I would much rather do that, Ma'am," Lady Bedstone replied. "I find getting in and out of carriages very tiring. And it was so hot walking round the garden."

"Then you rest in the shade," the Princess said in a comforting tone. "We will not be long."

The Vicar, the Reverend Patrick Grandell, was

waiting with the front door open when they got out of the Chaise.

He gave a very correct bow to the Princess as to Royalty, moving only his head and not his shoulders.

He did the same to the Prince, who shook him by the hand.

"My wife is waiting for you, Ma'am, in the Drawing-Room," he said to the Princess. "I thought perhaps His Royal Highness would like to come and look at my Bowling-Green, which I have just completed and also a target I have just erected for an Archery contest."

"I would very much like to see both," the Prince agreed.

The Vicar led him away across a small hall and opened a door on the other side of it.

"Her Royal Highness is here, Lycia," he said.

His wife, who had been sitting sewing in the window, hastily got to her feet.

The girl who was sitting beside her rose too.

When Princess Marigold looked at her, she gave a little gasp.

There was no doubt the Prince was right.

Although it seemed extraordinary, the daughter of the Vicar and his wife was indeed very like her.

She had the same fair hair, which was understandable, as the Vicar himself was fair-haired and blue-eyed.

But she had her Mother's dark Greek eyes that seemed almost too big for her small pointed face.

She was in fact, so like the Princess that it was uncanny.

She was, however, two years younger and there

was something about Avila's beauty that the Princess did not have.

There was, Prince Holden thought, something spiritual about her.

Something which made her seem not quite human, as if she belonged to a different world from that of the other people present.

As the Vicar's wife curtsied very gracefully, her daughter did the same.

Then the Vicar said in a jovial manner:

"His Royal Highness and I are going to leave you, Lycia. I was never a particularly good Linguist where Greek is concerned, and I rather suspect His Royal Highness finds it a difficult language to follow."

"I am afraid that is the truth," Prince Holden agreed. "My French and Italian are far better."

The Vicar laughed and shut the door.

Mrs. Grandell said politely in Greek:

"Would Your Royal Highness like to sit in the sunshine, or would you find it cooler on the sofa?"

She indicated one near the fireplace and the Princess moved towards it.

When she had sat down she said in a low voice:

"I have come to ask you for your help, Mrs. Grandell, and please do help me, because it is very, very important."

Mrs. Grandell, who was, the Princess decided, a beautiful woman with an unmistakable dignity about her, said in surprise:

"Of course! I should be delighted to help Your Royal Highness, if it is possible."

As if she thought she might be intruding, Avila began to walk towards the door.

"No, no, please stop," Princess Marigold said. "I

want you to hear what I have to say, because it concerns you."

Avila looked surprised, but she sat down in a chair beside her Mother's.

Quickly, because she thought she might not have too much time before the Vicar returned, Princess Marigold told Mrs. Grandell how she had fallen in love with Prince Holden.

She then explained how on the very day their engagement was to have been announced, they had been plunged into mourning.

"I will be frank with you," she said, "and explain that I am terrified, because Her Majesty the Queen wanted me to marry someone very important, that she will use any excuse to try to separate us."

Mrs. Grandell was listening with an astonished expression in her eyes.

"But, surely . . .?" she began.

"Let me finish," the Princess interrupted. "You may have heard of Prince Eumenus of Malia, who has just died. He is to be buried in Athens, and his body is being embalmed in order to give the important people of Europe time to attend the ceremony."

Princess Marigold had been watching Mrs. Grandell as she spoke.

She thought there was a flicker in her eyes which told her that she knew who Prince Eumenus was.

"Malia is, I believe, only a very small island, but Queen Victoria has decided I must represent her at the Funeral."

"Surely," Mrs. Grandell said a little tentatively, "Her Majesty could find someone older than Your

Royal Highness for what is inevitably a somewhat gloomy occasion?"

"She could, but she will not," Princess Marigold replied, "simply because she wishes to separate me from Prince Holden."

She clasped her hands together as she said:

"But I have fallen in love. I love him, Mrs. Grandell, as only you who are Greek can understand. If we are separated as Her Majesty is trying to do, I think it would kill me!"

She was speaking from her heart.

Her voice seemed to vibrate across the small room.

"I understand what you are feeling," Mrs. Grandell said quietly, "but I do not understand how I can help you."

"What I am asking," Princess Marigold said, "is if your daughter Avila will go to Athens in my place!"

Mrs. Grandell stared at the Princess as if she could not believe what she had heard.

Avila gave a little cry.

"Are you suggesting, Ma'am, that I could go to Greece?" she asked. "It is something I have always longed to do, ever since I was a child."

"I am asking you to impersonate me and go to Athens," the Princess said, "and to see, despite the Funeral Ceremony, as much of Greece as you can."

"This is the most wonderful thing that could possibly happen to me!" Avila cried.

Mrs. Grandell seemed at last to find her voice.

"Are you really serious, Ma'am?" she enquired. "I can hardly believe what Your Royal Highness is saying."

"I am saying that I am desperate!" Princess Marigold replied. "I know that if I go to Greece and leave Prince Holden, Her Majesty will somehow or other prevent our marriage from taking place, or at least delay it in some tricky way of her own."

She drew in her breath and went on:

"Please . . please, let Avila go instead of me! We look so alike that I am quite certain no one will have the slightest idea that she is not actually me!"

Mrs. Grandell turned to look at her daughter, then back again at the Princess.

"There is . . a definite . . resemblance," she admitted slowly.

"If we were not side by side, no one would doubt for a moment that Avila is me," the Princess said quickly. "I think in fact, we must be related in some way, as so many Greeks are."

To her surprise Mrs. Grandell stiffened.

"That, Ma'am," she said, "is something I do not wish to discuss. I admit there is a resemblance, but I am sure that my husband would not allow Avila to act a lie."

"Then you must not tell him," the Princess said. "As a Greek, you understand what I am feeling as no woman of any other nationality could. I can only beg you, plead with you, to help me, because this concerns my whole happiness, now and for the future."

"I do . . not know . . what to say," Mrs. Grandell murmured.

She had not moved or fidgeted while the Princess was talking.

Now she clasped her hands together almost as if they helped her to control her feelings.

"Oh, please, Mama, please!" Avila begged. "Let me go to Greece! You know how thrilled I have been by the stories you have told me ever since I was a baby, and the books we have read and the pictures we have found."

She paused before she went on:

"I never thought I would be able to see the Parthenon, or any of the islands of which you have told me so many stories. Please, Mama please! Let me do what Her Royal Highness asks!"

Princess Marigold thought the girl's pleading was even more impressive than her own.

Then, still speaking Greek, Mrs. Grandell said:

"Will you tell me, Your Royal Highness, how you think you can manage this . . deception without anyone being . . aware of it?"

Princess Marigold felt her heart leap.

"I will tell you what I have discussed so far with Prince Holden," she said, "and as he is a marvellous organiser, he will work out every detail so that there is not the slightest chance of our being discovered."

She saw the Mrs. Grandell was still undecided, and she went on:

"You must tell your husband that Avila is coming to Greece with me, which is almost true. Tell him I am taking her with me because, having lived in England for so long, I must practise my Greek and be certain I do not make any mistakes when I reach Athens."

She thought as she spoke that Mrs. Grandell thought this sounded at least a possible idea.

"It is quite true," she went on, "there is nobody at Windsor Castle with whom I can converse in Greek, and I have in fact become rather 'rusty' since my Father and Mother died. It was of course my Father who taught me first when I was a child."

"I am sure Papa would think it a wonderful opportunity," Avila said, "for me to go to Greece with Your Royal Highness."

"You will travel by ship," Princess Marigold said, "and I will choose a Lady-in-Waiting to accompany you who is getting old and also rather blind."

She stopped speaking for a moment, and then went on:

"She will, I expect, be the only other English person in the party, with the exception of the Under Secretary of State for Foreign Affairs, whom I have never met!"

She gave a little laugh as she said:

"I am sure they will expect me to remain in my cabin and feel sea-sick all through the Bay of Biscay, and when the ship reaches Athens, neither our Ambassador there, nor any of his Staff have ever met me."

"Prince Holden is not going with you?" Mrs. Grandell asked.

Princess Marigold shook her head.

"This is all a plot of Queen Victoria's to try to separate us," she said. "I am certain she is at this very moment working out in her mind how I will forget him, and he will forget me. But that is something that will never, ever happen!"

Now the anxious note was back in her voice.

There was something very pathetic in her eyes as she added:

"Please, please help me! There is no one else to whom I can turn, and only someone who is Greek can understand what I feel."

Avila looked at her Mother.

Then as Mrs. Grandell did not speak she put a hand over hers.

"Please, Mama, please," she begged. "We would be very careful not to upset Papa, and I promise I will do everything Her Royal Highness tells me to do."

"You just have to smile, keep saying 'Thank you', and wave to the crowds," the Princess said. "I can assure you, being a Royal person requires no brains, not unless you are in a spot like me, and have to try to save yourself."

Mrs. Grandell realised that both the Princess and her daughter were looking at her pleadingly.

In a strange tone that did not sound like her usual voice, she said:

"Because I would like Avila to see Greece, and because I am aware of the strange resemblance there is between her and Your Royal Highness, I will agree. But the only condition is that this is kept completely secret, and my husband is not aware of what is happening."

"I can assure you that from my point of view," the Princess answered, "no one must know except for us three and of course Prince Holden."

She smiled and then went on:

"I will rely on him to work out every move, every tiny detail, so that we are not discovered."

Mrs. Grandell did not speak and the Princess said as an afterthought:

"Avila and I are almost the same size and all that she will require is that dismal, boring black of which I have dozens and dozens of gowns! Besides, of course, the correct bonnet with a dark veil which will prevent anyone from looking too closely at her until she is aboard the battleship."

"And I can keep my head bent," Avila said, "as if it is such a moving occasion that I must not look too happy about it."

The Princess smiled.

"Exactly! I am sure you will act the part very, very well, and be much more charming and good-tempered than I would be!"

She gave a little laugh and went on:

"I would be hating every minute of the voyage, the Funeral, and the people who are preventing me from being with Prince Holden."

"While I will love every minute of it!" Avila said in a rapt voice. "Oh, thank you, thank you, Your Royal Highness, for thinking of me."

"You should really thank Prince Holden, who happened to see you in Church," Princess Marigold said. "But be very careful what you say to him if he is with your Father."

"You are not to say anything at all!" Mrs. Grandell said. "The sole reason, Your Royal Highness, that I am letting Avila go on what seems to me a rather dangerous and certainly very unusual journey is that she has always longed to see Greece."

She smiled and then said reflectively:

"It was my country, and I have wanted her to see it too. There is nowhere in the world that can compare with it!"

"That is what my Father always said," Princess Marigold agreed, "and it broke his heart when the Revolutionaries took away his throne."

"I suppose they were incited to rebellion by the Russians," Mrs. Grandell said. "They have caused trouble in so many of the Balkan States. I have heard recently that they have also been busy in Greece."

Princess Marigold had heard Queen Victoria's views on Russia's behaviour.

But she felt it unnecessary to become involved in that at the moment.

Instead she said:

"I know that Avila will love Greece, and I expect you have told her so many stories about it that she will feel as if she is going home rather than to a foreign country."

For the first time since they had started their conversation, Mrs. Grandell smiled at the Princess.

"You understand," she said softly.

"As Greeks," the Princess said, "we both know it is important for Avila to see Greece, and how better than being taken to everything that she asks to see because they believe she is me?"

"That is exactly what I was thinking," Mrs. Grandell said. "Yet I can only pray, Your Royal Highness, that our little plot will not be discovered. Because if it is, there will be a great number of people very angry with us."

"No one is more aware of that than I am," the Princess agreed. "I assure you, I shall be extremely careful and will not be happy until the Battleship moves out of port carrying Avila instead of me!"

Avila clasped her hands together.

"Oh, thank you, thank you, Ma'am!" she cried. "How can I ever tell you how grateful I am for this wonderful opportunity?"

She looked so pretty as she spoke that the Princess could not help saying:

"How is it possible that we look so alike? Surely,

Mrs. Grandell, you must be aware of some explanation for it?"

To her surprise, Mrs. Grandell rose to her feet.

"I think, Your Royal Highness," she said, "it would be a mistake to speak of anything except the task that lies ahead. I have a lot to teach Avila before she leaves, and a lot to tell her about Athens which is the one part of Greece she will certainly see."

"You must see everything else you can," the Princess said turning to Avila. "In a way I envy you. At the same time, even for the splendour of Greece, I cannot risk losing my future happiness."

She rose from the sofa as she spoke and put out her hand towards Mrs. Grandell.

"Thank you for being so understanding. I knew as soon as Prince Holden said you were Greek not only that we shared the same language, but also that we would understand each other without words."

It was a pretty speech, said with all the charm Princess Marigold could use when she chose to do so.

"Your Royal Highness is very kind," Mrs. Grandell said. "Avila and I will await your instructions, and carry them out to the letter."

"Thank you again," Princess Marigold said, "and now I must return to Windsor Castle to work out with Prince Holden every detail of what we have to do."

"And when do you expect to leave?" Mrs. Grandell asked.

"On Thursday," Princess Marigold replied. "It will be from Tilbury, and of course Prince Holden will send a carriage for you. I have not yet been told the name of the Battleship in which I am supposed to travel."

44

She saw the expression of delight in Avila's eyes as she spoke and said:

"That is something you will enjoy, and of course the Captain and the crew will be very proud to have been chosen to carry the Representative of Great Britain to Greece."

"I .. I think I .. must be .. dreaming!" Avila said. "This cannot .. really be .. happening to me!"

"It is," Princess Marigold said, "and when you listen to the long and dreary speeches which those who welcome you will make, you will find it very difficult not to yawn or go to sleep!"

Avila laughed, and it was a very pretty sound.

"I am sure, Ma'am, you are always clever enough to look as if you are enjoying it, however dull it may be."

"That is what I tell myself I should do," the Princess said, "but I warn you, old men can talk and talk for hours!"

Both Mrs. Grandell and Avila were laughing at this when the door opened.

"May we come in?" the Vicar asked, "or are you still dreaming you are living on Mount Olympus?"

"Of course that is where we are!" Princess Marigold replied. "For who could doubt that your daughter and I are goddesses?"

As she spoke she saw the expression in Prince Holden's eyes and knew that was how she appeared to him.

She felt a surge of love sweep over her.

"Even if Queen Victoria discovers our plot and punishes me," she told herself, "it will be worth the risk, if I can be with him!"

CHAPTER THREE

The *Traveller's Rest* at Tilbury was an Hotel where the guests never stayed long.

People arriving by sea might stay there temporarily, and people leaving in ships used it until they knew they could go aboard.

No one took any notice of a Lady who had engaged a room for herself and her daughter on Wednesday night.

She was in the Register as 'Mrs. Johnson'.

As soon as she and her daughter arrived, they went straight upstairs to their bedroom on the First Floor.

The following morning there was a rumble of excitement from those working in the Hotel.

They knew a party was arriving from Windsor Castle who would require coffee in the Private Lounge.

At a quarter after ten the first carriage arrived.

In it was Princess Marigold, and sitting beside her was Prince Holden.

Opposite them were Lady Bedstone and Colonel Bassett.

"I refuse to go aboard and do all that hand-

46

shaking until I have had a cup of coffee," Princess Marigold had said on the way.

"I thought that was what you would want," Prince Holden replied, "and I have already engaged a private room for you."

"The only other passengers, Ma'am," Colonel Bassett said, "will be Lord Cardiff, the Minister of State for Foreign Affairs, whom I do not think you have met, and the Greek Ambassador, who I believe is a charming man."

"In which case," Princess Marigold said, "I wonder why I have not been allowed to meet him before."

There was no answer to that and they drove on in silence until they reached the *Traveller's Rest*.

Prince Holden got out and helped the Princess alight.

They were greeted by the somewhat flurried Manager of the Hotel who escorted them to a Private Lounge.

The luggage had left Windsor Castle before the Princess.

It had been arranged that she should have a Greek Lady's-maid who was provided by the Greek Embassy.

There had been a little surprise about this at Windsor Castle, but the Princess had said:

"I am not going to be in a position where I cannot send my maid for anything I require or which has been forgotten, simply because she cannot speak the language."

She paused a moment and then went on:

"If I am going to Greece, I need a Greek

Lady's-maid, and preferably one who knows the shops in Athens."

No one felt inclined to argue about this.

The coffee was ready on the table for the Royal party.

The Princess, who was wearing the deepest black with a bonnet from which hung a long chiffon veil, accepted one of the sandwiches which Prince Holden offered her.

Then she asked:

"At what time are we due aboard?"

"The Captain wishes to sail at eleven o'clock," Prince Holden replied, "so I expect Colonel Bassett has arranged for us to arrive on the Quay at about a quarter to."

"That is what I planned we would do," Colonel Bassett said.

Lady Bedstone was taking pills with her coffee.

Princess Marigold knew she had received them from the Doctor just before she left.

They were a preventative against sea-sickness, but she was also sure that they would make Her Ladyship sleepy as well.

There had been further surprise among the Ladies at Windsor Castle that Lady Bedstone had been chosen for the journey.

But the Princess explained that she had asked for Lady Bedstone because she was retiring at the end of the Summer.

She also thought she would enjoy the rest during the voyage, both there and back.

No one could say this was not a kind thought, and Lady Bedstone had been very touched.

"The Princess may often be difficult," she said

to the other Ladies-in-Waiting, which was an under-statement, "at the same time, she has a kind heart."

The Princess, having drunk a little of her coffee now said:

"I am going upstairs to tidy myself. I believe you have engaged a room for me, Holden?"

"Yes, of course," the Prince replied. "I will find a maid to take you there."

They went from the Lounge together.

As the passage outside was deserted Prince Holden kissed her hand.

"Do not worry, my Darling," he whispered, "everything is going smoothly."

"Touch wood!" the Princess replied.

The Prince went into the main hall and found a maid to take Her Royal Highness upstairs.

A maid in a mob-cap and a gingham dress hurriedly obeyed.

The Princess was shown into a large double room.

"Be there anythin' Yer Royal 'Ighness wants?" the maid enquired.

"No, thank you," the Princess replied, "and you need not wait. I can find my own way downstairs."

The maid bobbed her a rather clumsy curtsy and went out, shutting the door behind her.

The Princess waited until she thought she must be out of ear-shot.

Then as Prince Holden had told her to do, she tapped on the wall on the right-hand side of the room.

As she did so she was praying that everything

had gone according to plan and that Avila would be there.

Two seconds later she slipped in through the door.

She was wearing a black gown that was very similar to the one the Princess had on.

But she had no bonnet on her shining golden hair.

Her eyes were excited and she looked so pretty that for a moment Princess Marigold felt almost jealous of her.

Avila dropped a curtsy.

'Is everythin' all right, Ma'am?" she asked.

"Everything so far," Princess Marigold answered.

As she spoke she took off the bonnet she was wearing and handed it to Avila.

It had been easy to provide her double with gowns.

But she had only one black bonnet.

She had been afraid it would cause a lot of comment if she ordered another.

Avila had arrived with her Mother, wearing her ordinary clothes and a hat trimmed with flowers.

The only item she had added, and which had been her own idea, was a pair of spectacles.

They had hidden the beauty of her eyes.

However with so many people coming and going in the Hotel, nobody had taken any notice of either her or her Mother.

She said now:

"I think I should tell Your Royal Highness that I wore the spectacles when I arrived, and perhaps it would be a good idea, Ma'am, for you to wear them when you leave."

"I will do that," Princess Marigold agreed, "and I hope your Mother has one of my own gowns ready for me next door."

"Yes, Ma'am, they arrived last night. We had just been praying that they had not been forgotten."

Avila went to the dressing-table to adjust the bonnet on her head and pull the chiffon veil over her face.

"Do I look all right, Ma'am?" she asked a little nervously.

"You look exactly like me!" the Princess assured her. "And do not forget when you go downstairs that you are feeling sad and upset at having to leave Prince Holden. Everyone will understand if you are not very talkative."

"Then . . shall I go . . now?" Avila asked as if she suddenly felt too helpless to make a decision herself.

The Princess looked at the clock that was on the mantelpiece.

"In another three minutes," she said, "and just in case anyone comes into this room and sees us together, I will go and join your Mother."

She put out her hand and laid it on Avila's shoulder.

"Thank you for doing this for me," she said. "I am very grateful and I hope you will have a lovely time in Greece."

Avila curtsied and Princess Marigold went towards the door.

She opened it cautiously and looked up and down the corridor.

It was empty and she swiftly moved into the room next door.

Mrs. Grandell was waiting for her and had one of the Princess's own summer gowns laid out on the bed.

Her Majesty the Queen had not called for Court mourning for Prince Eumenus. He was not important enough for that.

But she had said that she expected relations and Ladies-in-Waiting to wear black on the day of the Funeral.

Princess Marigold talked to Mrs. Grandell in Greek as she helped her into her pretty gown.

Then she put on the hat that was decorated to match it.

By the time she was dressed it was a few minutes to eleven o'clock.

She knew that by now the party downstairs would be going aboard *H.M.S. Heroic*.

This was the name of the Battleship that was to carry them to Athens.

The only person that she had been nervous about was Colonel Bassett.

If he guessed at the last minute that they were deceiving Queen Victoria, he might consider it his duty to inform Her Majesty of what they were doing.

Prince Holden had however thought of this.

Avila went up the gangway to be greeted with great respect by the Captain and three other Officers.

She was followed first by the Prince, then by Lady Bedstone.

After her came Lord Cardiff and finally, bringing up the rear were Colonel Bassett and the Greek Ambassador.

By the time he was greeting the Captain, Prince Holden had taken the Princess down the companionway.

A Steward led them to the cabins which had been allotted to Her Royal Highness for the voyage.

There was the one in which she was to sleep, where the Greek Lady's-maid from the Embassy was already busy unpacking her gowns.

Next to it was what had been the Captain's day-cabin.

This had been turned into a Sitting-Room for the Royal Party.

When they reached it, Prince Holden said:

"I think, as those following us will suppose we are saying good-bye to each other, there will be a slight delay before they join us."

He had left the door ajar and he looked back towards the companionway before he said:

"I think now I should go back and take Colonel Bassett away before he asks to say good-bye to you."

"That would be sensible," Avila replied, "and anyway I will go into my bed-cabin, so that no one except Lady Bedstone will follow me."

"You are quite safe where she is concerned," the Prince said. "She cannot see without using her lorgnettes, and invariably mislays them!"

Avila gave a little laugh before she said:

"I think all your arrangements have been mar-vellous, and I am so excited to be here that I am more grateful than I can say."

"And we are even more grateful to you," the Prince replied. "Take care of yourself and try not to be frightened."

Avila smiled at him through her veil.

Then as they heard footsteps on the companion-way she slipped into her cabin.

She began speaking in Greek to the maid who was hanging up her clothes.

The Prince went up above.

He found, as he expected, that the Captain was waiting somewhat impatiently for him and Colonel Bassett to leave.

Having shaken hands and wishing everyone a good voyage the Prince hurried down the gangway.

There were two closed carriages waiting on the Quay.

One was there to take Colonel Bassett back to Windsor Castle. The Prince's carriage was just near it.

"I thought I might offer Your Royal Highness a lift,' Colonel Bassett said as he followed him down the gangway.

"As it happens, I am going in the opposite direc-tion," Prince Holden replied, "but I will see you of course as soon as Her Royal Highness returns."

"I can only hope the Funeral is not as depress-ing as Her Royal Highness anticipates," Colonel Bassett answered.

"I hope so too," the Prince replied. "But you know only too well how these Funerals are conducted, and I am grateful that I do not have to be one of the mourners."

Colonel Bassett agreed and the Prince walked away and got into his own carriage.

He deliberately waited until Colonel Bassett had driven away and his carriage was out of sight.

Then he drove back to the *Traveller's Rest*, where he saw a closed carriage waiting for Mrs. Grandell.

He opened the door of his own carriage to alight.

Before he could do so Princess Marigold ran down the steps of the Hotel and jumped in beside him.

As the Prince put out his hands towards her the Coachman, who already had his orders, drove off to a different Quay.

It was some distance from the one where *H.M.S. Heroic* had been.

The horses moved slowly through piles of luggage, people boarding other ships, and a number of new arrivals.

The Princess flung herself against Prince Holden.

"We have .. done it! We have .. done .. it!" she cried.

Because Prince Holden was as excited as she was, he did not answer.

He drew her closer to him and kissed her.

Only when she could speak again did the Princess say:

"How can .. you have been .. so .. clever? How can you have been .. so wonderful as to work out .. everything .. so .. perfectly?"

She paused before she said in a different voice:

"No one on the ship was suspicious?"

"No one!" the Prince said triumphantly.

"And Colonel Bassett?"

"He hardly had a chance to get near to Avila, and did not speak to her. He has gone back to Windsor Castle, pleased with himself that he was able to make the Princess accept the Queen's instructions to go to Greece!"

The Princess gave a little laugh.

Then she said nervously:

"Let us get away from here quickly! I am so afraid that something will prevent us from doing so at the last minute!"

As she spoke the horses came to a standstill.

She looked out of the window to see the Prince's yacht moored to the Quay.

The Prince got out of the carriage first.

He helped the Princess to alight and escorted her up the gangway.

The Captain of the yacht was waiting for them and the Prince, who had seen him the previous day, merely said:

"Put to sea immediately, Captain Bruce."

The Captain bowed and the Prince drew Princess Marigold into the Saloon.

The yacht was large and comfortable.

The Saloon was attractively decorated, although in somewhat masculine taste.

There was a bottle of champagne waiting in a wine-cooler.

The Prince looked at Princess Marigold.

"Will you have a cup of coffee, or a glass of champagne?" he asked.

"Champagne, of course!" she answered. "We have so much to celebrate!"

"Very, very much to celebrate!" the Prince repeated.

The way he spoke made her look at him quickly.

"What in particular?" she asked.

"I will show you what I mean after you have had a glass of champagne and we go below."

"Now you are being mysterious," Princess Marigold protested.

The Prince poured out the champagne.

Then as Princes Marigold lifted her glass she gave a little cry.

"We are .. moving! We are .. moving! Oh, Holden, we have done it! We have escaped and now we can really enjoy ourselves without a boring Lady-in-Waiting, without the Statesmen, the Politicians, and without of course the watchful eye of Her Majesty the Queen!"

She put down her glass of champagne for a moment and pulling off her hat threw it on a chair.

"We are free! We are free for two weeks or more," she cried, "and I want them to be the happiest days you have ever spent."

"I have made sure of *that*," the Prince replied.

There was an intonation in the way he spoke which made the Princess look at him questioningly.

"Drink your champagne," he said. "I have something to show you."

"You are making me curious!" the Princess complained. "I only hope it is not a surprise that will frighten me!"

"I hope not!" the Prince smiled.

Princess Marigold finished her glass of champagne.

By this time, the yacht was moving out of the Dock and into the estuary.

The sun was shining and shimmering on the water.

For a moment she just stood looking out of the port-holes in the Saloon.

Then she said:

"You have not yet told me where we are going."

"I want you to believe it is to Heaven," the Prince replied. "Now come and see what I have to show you."

Mystified, the Princess took his hand and they went down the companionway together.

The yacht was a new model and equipped with all the latest devices.

They walked towards the stern where Princess Marigold knew the Master Cabin would be.

She thought questioningly there was a serious expression in the Prince's eyes.

"Surely, nothing can have gone wrong?" she asked herself.

Suddenly she was afraid in case he had brought someone else with them.

She knew if he had done so it would spoil all her joy at being alone with him.

The Prince opened the door of the Master cabin.

There was a large bed which traditionally was a four-poster draped with curtains.

There was however no one in the cabin.

Because she had been afraid there might be, the Princess gave a sigh of relief.

Then she was aware that lying on the bed there was a large bouquet of white flowers.

Beside it was a wreath of white orchids.

She looked at them, then she asked:

"Are these for . . me?"

"They are for my bride!" the Prince answered.

The Princess stared at him.

"We are being married, my Darling," he said, "just as soon as we are further out to sea. It will be a marriage performed by my Captain which is entirely legal and no one can ever take you from me."

For a moment the Princess was too astonished to speak.

Then as he waited, she flung her arms around him.

"Oh, Holden . . Holden, how can you think of anything so . . wonderful?"

The Prince held her tightly against him.

"I knew," he said, "that I could not damage your reputation, my Lovely One, and it would have been impossible for me to be alone with you for so long without making you mine."

His voice deepened as he went on:

"I want you, and God knows, I have waited long enough! Now I am making sure that whatever happens in the future, nothing shall ever separate us."

"Oh, Holden, it is what I want too!" the Princess cried. "But I never thought of our being married at sea."

"If our plot remains undiscovered," the Prince said, "we can be married again with all the pomp and ceremony which you, like all women, will enjoy. But this, our secret marriage, will be absolutely binding."

He paused before he said in a different voice:

"If the worst comes to the worst, and the Queen discovers what has happened, there will be nothing by the laws of England, or the laws of my country, that she can do about it."

"That is what I want, that is exactly what I want!" the Princess murmured.

If the Prince had wanted to say any more, it would have been impossible.

She pulled his head down to hers and pressed her lips against his.

She kissed him with a happiness that seemed to light the whole cabin with their love.

. . . .

On board *H.M.S. Heroic* Avila took off her black bonnet and tidied her hair.

Feeling a little nervous, but at the same time excited, she went into the cabin next door.

The Greek Ambassador and Lord Cardiff were there and they rose to their feet when she entered.

They were both, she saw, drinking a glass of sherry.

As she asked them to sit down again the Ambassador began to pay her compliments.

He was speaking in his own language and was delighted when she replied with a fluency he had not expected.

It was only after they had been chatting for some time that Avila remembered they were being rude to Lord Cardiff.

"I must apologise, My Lord," she said in English, "but I need to polish up my Greek before I reach Athens, so that I do not miss anything that is said. Just as I have no wish to miss anything I can see."

Lord Cardiff laughed.

"I am afraid my Greek, Ma'am, which I learnt at School is not, shall we say, very conversational. However, I can usually manage to obtain what I want in Restaurants and in shops."

"That is a step in the right direction!" Avila smiled. "You will understand how exciting it will be for me to be in the country to which I half-belong, and to hear the people speak a language which is not often heard in England."

"When we return," the Ambassador said, "I shall make certain that Your Royal Highness is notified of everything that takes place at the Embassy. I realise now that we have been very remiss in not asking you to attend when we have exhibitions of Greek dancing, and Greek Lec-turers who talk about the ancient history of Greece and its ruins."

"I would love that!" Avila replied enthusi-astically.

Then she remembered that it would be Princess Marigold, not she, who would be invited to England.

She talked a great deal to the Ambassador about the Temples that were still standing in Delphi and the Parthenon in Athens.

They also spoke about the many beautiful relics that could be found on the different islands.

"You certainly know more about Greece,

Ma'am, than I ever expected!" he said that night at dinner.

"And I never expected to see what I have only read about," Avila replied.

"You do not remember much about the country before your Father and Mother came to England?" the Ambassador asked.

With a little throb of fear, Avila realised she had made a mistake!

It was something she must never do again.

She tried desperately to remember what she had been told about Princess Marigold's early life.

"I am afraid," she said after a pause, "I actually remember very little about it. I was only four years old at the time but I can recall the garden where I played, and the delightful room, which I think must have been my Nursery."

"If only you had been a little older," the Ambassador sighed. "But never mind, we can make up for it now, and I know, because you have Greek blood in your veins, you will find everywhere you look there is something that pulls at your heart, and at the same time invigorates your mind."

It was something which had never been said to Avila before.

It made her feel even more excited than she was already.

She would see Greece and feel the light which her Mother had told her had eventually enveloped the world.

It was a light that not only dazzled the eyes, but which made the Greeks give the civilised world the power to think, to plan and to create.

． ． ． ． ． ． ．

That night, when she went to bed in her cabin, Avila said:

"Thank You God, for letting me come on this wonderful voyage of discovery. Forgive me for deceiving Papa, and let me find in Greece the answer to all the questions that have puzzled me."

It was a very sincere prayer.

Then she snuggled down against her soft pillows and felt the ship's engines turning beneath her.

She was thinking how fortunate she was.

A new world was opening out before her, a world that was part of her blood.

She knew it was also part of her heart and her soul.

'Greece, the Gateway of the Mind'.

The Light which had been first lit by the God of Light himself – Apollo!

CHAPTER FOUR

As they steamed through the Mediterranean Avila knew she had never enjoyed herself so much.

Ever since they left Tilbury, Lady Bedstone had remained in her cabin.

She had refused to move until they had passed through the Bay of Biscay.

This meant that Avila had the two elderly men to herself.

They complimented and praised her, and talked to her about all the things which she found interesting.

At first it seemed strange to be addressed as 'Your Royal Highness' or 'Ma'am', but she soon grew used to it.

At the same time, she could not help wishing that her Mother was with her.

She knew how much she would have enjoyed listening to the Ambassador.

Avila learnt things about Greece she had never known before and was wildly excited when they reached Athens.

H.M.S. Heroic steamed into Port at exactly the expected time of arrival, which was midday.

The Quay at which they docked was decorated with a profusion of Greek flags and Union Jacks.

As Avila looked down at the crowd the Ambassador said:

"I can see the Prime Minister, so be prepared for a lengthy welcome."

"At last I am really in Greece!" Avila said in a rapt tone.

In the distance she could see the Sacred Rock of the Acropolis with the Parthenon on the top of it.

Because it was so exciting, she wanted to clap her hands and cheer.

Then she was aware that seeing her on deck the people on the Quay were waving and shouting 'Welcome!' in Greek.

The Ambassador led her down the gangway.

As he had warned her, the Prime Minister was there to greet her, together with a number of other Statesmen.

Avila was given a large bouquet of flowers.

There were three speeches of welcome, each longer than the last.

Avila was delighted that she was able to understand every word they said.

Then in an open carriage she was driven to the British Embassy where she was to stay.

The Ambassador had already explained to her that it had been first thought that she would not be staying at the Palace since the King was away, visiting his relations in Denmark.

It was one thing, Avila thought, to deceive the Ambassador and the Prime Minister that she was a 'Royal Highness'.

It was quite another to deceive a King.

She was well aware, because her Mother had told her, of the difficulties there had been in Greece, after they had deposed King Otto.

At last they had found the King they required.

There were a number of candidates.

Finally the search had ended with William, the seventeen-year-old second son of the heir to the throne of Denmark.

The Treaty of Accession had been signed in London twenty-three years ago in 1863 by the representatives of Great Britain, France, Austria, Prussia and Russia.

The new King took the title of 'George I of the Hellenes'.

It had been easy to sign a contract.

But difficult to win the acceptance of the many Principalities and leading Greek families.

They all had their own importance and wished to keep the power they had held over the centuries.

Avila was glad she did not have to listen to the many problems and squabbles which had ensued.

The British Embassy was a large, delightful building set in a large garden.

The British Ambassador welcomed her with yet another speech, but not such a long one.

He explained that his wife was unfortunately away, which Avila thought was a relief.

A woman, she thought, was far more likely than a man to notice if she did or said anything wrong.

Avila was therefore chaperoned by Lady Bedstone, who made a tremendous effort to be charming to everyone and even tried to speak a few words of Greek.

The Funeral, they learned was to take place the next day.

Avila wondered if she could say there were sights she would like to see that afternoon.

It was then that the Greek Ambassador said:

"I think I should explain to Your Royal Highness that the deceased Prince Eumenus had no sons. His nephew His Royal Highness Prince Darius of Kanidos will therefore be looking after you and I am only surprised that he is not here already."

"His Royal Highness did say," a member of his staff who had joined them interposed, "that he had to see the Priest about the Funeral Service, and might be late."

"Oh, yes, of course," the Ambassador agreed, "I had forgotten."

Even as he spoke a servant announced:

"His Royal Highness Prince Darius of Kanidos!"

Avila turned to see the Prince coming into the room.

He was certainly very good-looking.

In fact as he advanced towards her she could not help thinking that he might have been the model for a statue of Apollo.

He had perfectly chiselled features.

Her Mother had told Avila these were characteristic of the aristocratic Greeks.

He also had the lithe physique of an athlete.

His dark eyes somehow resembled her own.

As he came nearer Avila realised that he was looking at her searchingly as well as with an expression of surprise.

"Let me present, Your Royal Highness," the British Ambassador was saying, "Prince Darius of Kanidos who will be delighted to show you all the famous sights of Athens."

Avila put out her hand.

When the Prince took it she felt strange vibrations from his fingers.

It made her think that he was even more like a god than he had appeared.

She remembered that when Apollo poured across the sky, flashing with a million points of light, healing everything he touched, he germinated the seeds and defied the Powers of Darkness.

She did not know why that particular description came into her mind.

But it came vividly as the Prince held her hand in his.

Almost as if he was speaking to himself he said:

"You are even more beautiful than I expected you to be!"

Avila blushed and he added:

"I was told to show you the beauties of Athens, but now I want Athens to see you!"

It sounded different in Greek from how it would have sounded in English.

Avila thought no one had ever said anything so wonderful to her before.

When they went into luncheon, the Prince was seated on her right.

He asked her what she wanted particularly to see while she was staying in Greece.

"Everything!" she demanded. "I cannot believe I am really here! I have read about Greece, talked about it, but thought I would never actually be able to see it as I can now."

There was no mistaking the enthusiasm in her voice.

The Prince said quietly:

"I believe you are here only for a short time, but I promise you I will not allow you to waste a minute. This afternoon I will take you first to the Parthenon."

Avila gave a little cry of delight.

"I saw it! I could see it from the ship as we came into Port!" she said. "It looked exactly as I always believed it would!"

"We will go there as soon as we have finished luncheon," the Prince said, "but you must remember that nobody hurries in Athens."

He smiled before he added:

"The women walk slowly and gracefully, and the Cafés are full of men gossiping."

Avila laughed.

"But I shall have to hurry," she said. "Otherwise, how else am I to see everything in Greece before the ship carries me back to England?"

"I have a feeling there are to be more speeches to listen to when luncheon is finished, but with your permission, I will suggest they are kept until after dinner tonight when it will be too dark to show you the beauty of Athens."

"Oh, yes, please do that," Avila begged.

Because she was so excited she grudged the time they took to eat the delicious food they were offered.

As the Prince had suggested, he asked the

Ambassador that there should be no speeches until this evening.

"Her Royal Highness wishes to see the whole of Greece," he said, "but as that is impossible, I have to show her at least the most beautiful places before she returns to her own country."

There was a murmur of agreement at this.

Finally, even sooner than Avila had anticipated, they had left the Embassy and were moving in an open carriage along the road which led to the Acropolis.

Lady Bedstone had to go with them.

Avila however, told her in a whisper that she was to stay in the carriage and not to try to walk up to the Parthenon on the summit of the Acropolis.

Lady Bedstone was only too delighted to stay where she was.

As she had enjoyed the luncheon, Avila was certain that, if she had the opportunity, she would drop off to sleep.

The horses climbed as far as they could up to the great entrance portal of the Acropolis.

Then the Prince sprang out and held out his hand to Avila.

Again she felt that strange vibration.

It seemed in some way she did not understand, to link her with him.

The Parthenon was even grander and more impressive than she had imagined.

It rose above the purple rock like a great ship with all its sails flying.

"That is what I have always thought," the Prince said quietly.

She turned to look at him.

"You are reading my thoughts!"

"I realised at luncheon that was what I could do," the Prince said. "I cannot explain it, but why should we want to?"

There was something in the way he looked at Avila that made her feel strange.

Because she also felt shy, she began to ask him questions.

He told her how the marble of the Parthenon had been painted with colour, blue, scarlet and gold.

"Today however," he said quietly, "we see it as the Greeks saw it perhaps about 440 B.C. shortly before it was finished."

They wandered among its many columns and the Prince quoted the words of Pericles.

He had said that the Parthenon was built so 'the heart may be warmed and the eye delighted for ever'.

"That is what has happened," Avila said. "One cannot help looking at it and being delighted. At the same time, it makes me feel small and unimportant."

"That is something you could never be," the Prince said.

He then took her to the Erechtheion.

The six figures had been sculpted in the form of beautiful maidens, a rare but lovely form of architecture.

The Prince then told her that columns sculpted in this way were known as Karyatids. The word meant maidens of the little country town of Karyar.

They were noted for performing ritual dances in which they sometimes posed in this attitude.

Avila stood looking at them thinking how beautiful and at the same time mysterious they were.

Then she became aware that the Prince was looking at her.

She felt the Erechtheion had a strange feeling of sanctity about it.

As if the Prince was again reading her thoughts, he said:

"The sacred robe of Athene was preserved here. It was here too that the golden lamp was never allowed to go out."

"I wish I could have seen Athene!" Avila said.

"*I am* seeing her!" the Prince answered.

She looked at him in surprise.

Then when she realised what he meant, she blushed.

"This is the right place for you," he said softly. "While the Parthenon is masculine, the Erechtheion is wholly feminine. I feel sure that you have been here before, and as Athene, belonged to the light, so do you."

Avila drew in her breath.

She could hardly believe that anyone was saying to her things she had thought of only in her dreams.

When she had read about the gods and goddesses she had imagined she herself was one of them.

She knew that nothing could be more complimentary than that the Prince should think of her in the same breath as Athene.

Then very quietly he said:

"Athene meant so much to the Ancient Greeks and she was worshipped under so many conflicting aspects."

His voice deepened as he went on:

"There was Athene the Warrior, shaking her spear, Athene the Companion, and Athene of the Household. She was the goddess of all things fair, and she was also Athene the Virgin, determined to protect the virginity of her city."

"That is . . beautiful . . the way you say it," Avila murmured.

There was a little pause before the Prince replied:

"There was also Athene the Goddess of Love. I always think of these maidens whom we have just been admiring as if they were priestesses of Athene as Goddess of Love."

He looked down at Avila and added:

"Now I know why I have always been drawn to the Erechtheion more than to the Parthenon itself."

Avila felt that if he said any more, it might spoil the wonder of what had already been spoken.

She therefore started to walk down towards the carriage.

The Prince moved beside her without protest.

She knew it was because once again he had been reading her thoughts.

"How is it possible," she asked herself, "that he can know what I am thinking?"

Yet she was aware that they were speaking without words.

It was so strange, so unexpected, that she felt frightened.

Then as they neared the carriage the Prince said softly:

"Do not be afraid. Because you are Greek you will hear things that other people do not hear, and see things that other people do not see. They are all part of the wonder and glory of this marvellous land which has a Divine radiance for those who belong to it."

They reached the carriage and Lady Bedstone who had been asleep, woke up.

"I hope you have enjoyed yourselves," she remarked.

It was then that Avila felt she had been brought back to reality from another world.

. . . .

They dined early.

The English Ambassador had invited a large party to meet, as they supposed, Her Royal Highness the Princess Marigold.

There were a number of pleasant young Greek men, but somehow they did not compare with the Prince.

Even when he was at the other end of the room Avila was acutely aware of him.

Because he was so handsome she found it impossible not to keep thinking of him as Apollo.

She could also feel him vibrating towards her, so that it was difficult to follow the conversation of anyone who was speaking to her.

At one moment during the evening she went to the window.

She wanted to see the lights that were gleaming in every window within sight.

The stars were twinkling above the Parthenon.

Her Mother had told her how the Greeks loved light.

They never tired of describing the appearance of it.

"They like the glitter of stones and sand washed by the sea," Mrs. Grandell said, "of fish churning in the nets, and they chose for the site of a Temple to Apollo twin cliffs which are called 'The Shining Ones'."

'I would love to go to Delphi,' Avila thought now, but she was sure it was too far away.

If she went, she knew she would want to see Delphi with Prince Darius walking beside her.

Even as she thought of him she was aware that he had joined her at the window.

"No other people but the Greeks," he said quietly, "leave so many lights burning at night. Light is their protection against the evil dark."

"I have heard that," Avila murmured.

She looked up at him, and he said:

"The Ancient Greeks understood the depth of darkness in the human soul, and they believed that at night their soul was at the mercy of their evil imaginings."

"I suppose too, they were very superstitious," Avila said.

"They refused to allow superstition to ride roughshod over them," the Prince replied, "and they believed, as I do, that the light of the mind can put an end to the darkness of the soul."

Avila stared at him.

She thought it a very strange conversation to be having with a young man.

Yet it was the sort of thing she had talked about with her Mother, and sometimes, in a rather different way, with her Father.

"You have come to see Greece," the Prince went on, "but in fact you already know the answers to the things which have puzzled your mind, and which you questioned before you came here."

"How do you know that?" Avila asked.

"Because only a Greek can understand Greece, and I knew this afternoon, as I know now, there is really nothing that I need explain to you. For the answer is there already in your heart, and of course your soul."

As he finished speaking, their eyes met.

Suddenly to her surprise, he turned without another word and walked away from her.

He left the room and for a moment she could not believe he had actually gone.

He did not return, and she felt that the room seemed empty.

Suddenly the light had disappeared, and there was a darkness she could not explain.

An hour later she went up to bed.

She was thinking that despite all the talks with her Mother and the books she had read, she had come nearer to understanding Greece in these last few hours than she ever had before.

She owed it, she knew, to the Prince who had suddenly left her as if he were indeed Apollo.

Perhaps he was already 'driving his chariot across the sky' to another part of the world.

"I will I see him again tomorrow," Avila told herself before she went to sleep.

· · · · · · ·

Prince Holden's yacht was anchored in a little bay along the French coast.

The marriage had taken place as soon as the yacht was in the English Channel.

Princess Marigold had worn the white gown, the wreath of orchids on her head, and carried the bouquet.

She had gone to the Saloon where Captain Bruce was waiting to perform the Marriage Ceremony.

He was looking very smart in his uniform and wearing his medals.

Prince Holden was already there, wearing, as was correct on the Continent, evening-dress.

There were several Orders sparkling with diamonds pinned to the breast of his cut-away coat.

A star on a red ribbon showed from under his cravat.

Taking Princess Marigold's hand, he stood with her before the Captain, who was holding a Prayer-Book.

Then he began the Marriage Service.

He married them according to the rights that were given to every ship's Captain.

It had been made law that a Captain could marry legally at sea any of those travelling in the ship which he commanded.

To Princess Marigold, the words were just as moving as if her wedding were taking place in St. Paul's Cathedral.

When finally Captain Bruce pronounced them man and wife, she felt as if there were angels singing overhead.

The Captain gave them his good wishes and left them alone together.

It was then Princess Marigold turned towards Prince Holden and said:

"We are married! We are really married, and now I am your wife!"

"Do you suppose, my Darling, that I am not aware of that?" he asked.

He put his arms around her and looked down at her with a serious expression in his eyes.

"You are mine!" he said. "My wife, and now no one can take you from me! At the same time, I swear before God that I will do everything in my power to make you happy and make sure you never regret giving yourself to me."

"It is . . the most . . wonderful thing that . . ever happened to . . me," Princess Marigold said, ". . . and the reason why I did not . . accept anyone else was that I knew that somewhere in the world there was you, and I . . belonged to . . you."

"Perhaps in many lives before this," the Prince said. "Personally, I am completely and utterly content that we are now together, whatever the difficulties in the future."

"There will be none!" Princess Marigold declared. "I feel the gods are with us, the gods of Greece, in whom my Father believed, and who have guarded me and brought you into . . my life."

"That is what I believe too," the Prince said. "My Darling, I am the luckiest and most fortunate man in the whole world!"

He pulled her against him and kissed her until the Saloon swung round them.

Then he raised his head and said:

"We are married, my Precious, and because I want to make sure of it, let us go below."

"We will .. do that," the Princess agreed, "and do you realise .. my wonderful Husband .. that nobody can interrupt us? There are no Equerries .. no Aides-de-Camp outside the door, no Ladies-in-Waiting making certain I am not alone with you."

She laughed and added:

"And for the moment no disagreeable Queen, determined to separate us."

Prince Holden kissed her forehead.

"Not even Queen Victoria can do that now, and as you agreed, my beautiful wife, let us go where we will not be interrupted."

They went below.

The sunshine was coming through the portholes of the Master Cabin.

It dazzled Princess Marigold's eyes, and glinted on her golden hair.

The Prince locked the door.

Then as they looked at each other they realised how fundamentally they had revolted against protocol.

In fact, against everything they had both been brought up to revere and observe.

They had started a revolution all of their own, and now, for the moment, were triumphantly free.

The Princess threw out her arms.

As the Prince held her against him they were both aware that they had fought a battle against what had seemed overwhelming odds, and emerged victorious.

. . . .

A long time later, Princess Marigold stirred against her husband's shoulder.

"My Precious, my Darling!" he said. "I have not hurt or frightened you?"

"W.why did you not . . tell me before that . . love was so . . w.wonderful?" the Princess asked. "I felt as if it . . carried me up to the sky . . and I . . touched . . the stars."

"That is what I wanted you to feel," the Prince said.

There had been a number of women in his life.

But he had never known anyone who could evoke in him the rapture that he felt with the Princess.

He knew it was because they felt for each other the real love that all men seek, but seldom find.

It was the love of the mind as well as the body: the soul as well as the heart.

He had known from the moment he first saw the Princess that she was everything he desired and wanted as his wife.

Yet she was important.

He was only a very minor Royal compared to her and he had thought it would be impossible ever to claim her for his own.

Now, by the mercy of God and a great deal of scheming on his part, they had managed to escape from the prison of convention into a world of their own.

He could hardly believe it possible.

It had persisted in his thoughts by day and by night that they must be together.

Not only for the two weeks of what he knew would be a blissful honeymoon.

But for the rest of their lives.

He was certain there would be difficulties about that.

Without doubt they would both suffer for the deception they had perpetrated if it was discovered.

He told himself however, it would be well worth it for the happiness they were feeling now.

The happiness he had been desperately afraid would elude him.

"Are you .. thinking of .. me?" the Princess asked in a soft little voice.

"How could I think of anything else?" the Prince asked. "Actually I was thanking God that we have been so fortunate as to get away without being stopped, to be married without being prevented and to know that, hard though the future may be, this moment is ours!"

He kissed her eyes as he spoke.

Then, because she lifted her mouth to his, he kissed her lips.

He felt the fire moving within them both.

He told himself that anything that happened in the future was unimportant beside what was happening now, at this moment.

Then the flames that were leaping higher and higher encompassed them both . . . . .

CHAPTER FIVE

The Funeral was very impressive in the little but charming early Byzantine Kapnikarea Church.

Built in the 10th Century in the shape of a cross, its cupola was supported by four columns.

Avila found herself responding to the beauty of the music, the fragrance of the incense and the seven silver lights hanging in front of the screen behind which lay the sanctuary.

The coffin had flowers piled round it.

Prince Darius had told Avila that anyone of any importance in Athens would come to the Funeral.

She was glad she had her black bonnet with its long veil over her face.

She could look at the people around her without their being able to see her at all closely.

She had never heard a Choir singing in Greek before, and she thought the beauty of the words matched the music.

When finally the service came to an end, everyone filed past the coffin and bent over to kiss the dead man's cheek.

Prince Darius escorted Avila out first before anyone else left.

She had learnt that King George was not

coming to the Funeral as he was in Denmark with his family.

She thought that the Prince and the Officials were rather relieved that there was not more protocol to attend to.

She walked out in silence beside Prince Darius, thinking how exceedingly smart he looked.

Lady Bedstone, who had sat at the back of the Church at her own request, was standing by the closed carriage which was waiting outside, when Avila reached it.

When the Prince handed her into it he said in a low voice:

"I am picking you up after luncheon. The Ambassador will tell you what I have planned."

She smiled at him through her veil and then the carriage drove away.

Now when they were alone, Avila lifted her veil and threw it back over her bonnet.

"Have you heard what is being planned for this afternoon?" she enquired.

"His Excellency did say that you were going somewhere," Lady Bedstone said vaguely. "I am afraid that I did not hear where it was."

They drove on to the Embassy.

The Prince had told her yesterday that an official luncheon was being given for the relatives and very close friends of the deceased, which he had to attend.

He thought she would find it rather boring, so she was to have luncheon in the Embassy.

She kept wondering now where he would take her after luncheon.

There was so much she wanted to see, but she

knew despondently that there was only one full day left before they must return to England.

Lord Cardiff had made this very clear when he said:

"I know, Ma'am, that you will understand that I have so many duties in England that I cannot afford to be away longer than is absolutely necessary."

It was with difficulty that Avila had not replied that she had plenty of time on her hands as far as Greece was concerned.

She would have liked to stay for weeks to see everything there was to be seen.

Now as they reached the British Embassy and she saw the Union Flag flying outside, she knew that she wanted to stay, not only to see more of Greece, but also to stay longer with the Prince.

She could not imagine there could be anything more fascinating than to hear him telling her about the gods and goddesses.

Explaining to her as he had yesterday the secrets of the Parthenon and the Erechtheion.

"I have one more day," she said to herself as the sentries saluted her when she went into the Embassy.

It was quite a small party at luncheon.

The Ambassador talked most of the time with Lord Cardiff about the situation in the Balkans.

Avila could not help thinking that she had never known an hour pass more slowly.

When luncheon was ended and she went into the Drawing-Room with Lady Bedstone she thought despairingly that time was being wasted when she might be sightseeing.

Then the British Ambassador came into the room rather hurriedly.

"I am so sorry, Your Royal Highness," he said apologetically, "I quite forgot what Prince Darius asked me to tell you."

For one moment Avila thought the Prince was not coming to see her after all, and she felt her heart drop.

"As he is anxious for you to see his house," the Ambassador went on, "and also, I understand, one of the islands tomorrow, he has suggested that you and Lady Bedstone should stay the night with him."

Avila gave a little murmur of excitement as the Ambassador went on:

"I am sure you will be impressed with Kanidos which is a very beautiful part of Greece. The Prince's house is not very far from here along the coast road leading South to Cape Sounion."

He paused a moment and then went on:

"This, as I am sure you know, is the most southerly point of Attica, the comparatively small area of which in Classical times Athens was the capital."

"I should love to see the Prince's house," Avila said.

"It is certainly very impressive," the Ambassador replied, "and I expect your maid will have already packed your clothes."

"What time are we leaving?" Avila asked.

"The Prince will be calling for you," the Ambassador answered, "as soon as his luncheon is finished. These 'wakes' as they call them in Scotland, usually go on for hours."

He smiled at her before continuing:

"But I am sure the Prince will be able to excuse himself. I should think he will be here very soon."

To Avila this was splendid news.

She went straight upstairs to her room, to find as the Ambassador had said, that her Greek maid had already packed her trunk.

She did however, change out of the elaborate and rather thick dress she had worn to the Funeral into something lighter.

Because the sun was shining she was only sorry that she could not wear one of the pretty muslin gowns she wore at home.

She looked at herself in the mirror somewhat despairingly.

She was not aware that black in fact, accentuated the transparency of her skin and made her hair appear even more golden than usual.

"Have I really got to wear this bonnet with its crêpe veil?" she asked herself.

She knew the answer: 'mourning is mourning', especially when it had anything to do with Queen Victoria.

Avila had only just finished getting ready when a servant announced that His Royal Highness was downstairs.

It was with difficulty that she managed to walk down slowly with what she hoped was dignity.

The Prince was waiting for her in the Drawing-Room.

He had changed from the conventional clothes he had worn in the morning.

"I have only just been told by His Excellency that we are to stay with you tonight," Avila said.

"It is something I am very much looking forward to."

"Not as much as I am," the Prince answered. "The carriages are outside."

"The carriages?" Avila questioned.

"Lady Bedstone told me that she preferred travelling in a closed carriage, while I thought you would like to see the countryside through which we shall be passing."

"Of course I would!" Avila exclaimed.

She spoke so fervently that she thought perhaps she was being indiscreet.

There was, she suspected, a twinkle in the Prince's eyes.

However as she was in a hurry to get away they went straight out to where the carriages were waiting.

She found the Prince had a Chaise in which he was driving her.

It was not unlike the one that Prince Holden drove, but slightly more elaborate.

It was also, Avila found, very comfortable.

The Prince helped her in and the Ambassador waved them goodbye.

The Chaise was drawn by two horses which were perfectly matched.

Avila knew they were well-bred, and they drew them out of Athens very quickly.

To begin with they drove almost in silence.

When there was no longer any traffic and the country in all its loveliness was on either side of them, Avila said:

"I was wondering this morning what you had

planned for me. I had no idea it would be as exciting as this."

"That is what I wanted you to feel," the Prince said. "I know how very little time we have."

He emphasised the word 'we'.

Avila replied:

"I feel perhaps I should not take you away from your Uncle's Funeral."

"I have left a number of relatives to act as hosts to the other mourners," the Prince said. "I have so much to show you in so short a time that we must not miss a second of it."

"That is what I have been thinking," Avila agreed.

She was aware that the Prince was a very good driver.

She had never seen anything so lovely as when a little later they had the sea on one side of them and the land green with the leaves of Spring on the other.

There were mountains in the distance and there seemed to be very few inhabitants.

Avila thought they were alone in a magical world which belonged to the gods of Greece.

"Another time," the Prince said, "I will take you to Delphi. But tomorrow I have another rather special place to take you to, which I feel you will appreciate because you are Greek, and because to Greeks it is the most sacred place in the world."

Avila looked at him in surprise wondering what he meant and then he said:

"I shall keep it a secret until tomorrow. Today I want you to concentrate on me. We are now in my territory which my family has reigned over for many generations."

It was certainly exceedingly beautiful with its Olive trees and distant mountains.

It was nearly two hours before Avila saw ahead of them a large building that was gleaming white in the sunshine.

For a moment she thought it must be a Temple.

Then as the Prince drove nearer towards it she asked:

"Is that your house?"

"It is," he replied, "and you will find it, in every way, very Greek."

"It looks like a Palace," Avila said as they drew nearer and she saw how large it was.

"It was originally built as one," the Prince explained. "We were Kings in mediaeval times when Greece consisted of a number of small kingdoms which were usually at war with one another."

"And now?" Avila asked.

"We hope, if the Russians leave us alone, to remain happily and prosperously united under our one King."

"I am sure your gods will help you to obtain your heart's desire," Avila said.

"That is what I am hoping they will do for me," the Prince said quickly.

There was a meaning in his voice which she could not misunderstand.

She blushed a little and deliberately looked ahead of her, hoping he would not notice.

"You are very lovely," the Prince said softly. "But I am going to talk about that tomorrow!"

Avila longed to know why he had to wait until tomorrow.

But she knew it was a question she could not ask him.

They were also drawing nearer and nearer to the beautiful house ahead.

And now with its Ionic columns and exquisite proportions it looked even more like a temple than when she had first seen it.

The Prince drew his horses to a standstill with a flourish.

Servants came hurrying out of the main door to greet them.

Lady Bedstone was not far behind.

By the time Avila had taken off her bonnet and tidied her hair her Lady-in-Waiting and her lady's-maid had come upstairs.

"I hope the journey was not too tiring for you," Avila said to Lady Bedstone.

"To be honest, Ma'am," Lady Bedstone replied, "I slept most of the way. The carriage was so comfortable that it really lulled me to sleep."

She yawned before she said:

"I hope Your Royal Highness will understand that now we have arrived I would like to rest. Then I will not be too tired to come down to dinner."

"Yes, of course," Avila agreed. "As soon as you are unpacked I should get into bed. I am sure if you would like a cup of tea someone will bring it to you."

She saw the relief on the old lady's face and hurried downstairs.

The Prince was alone in one of the most beautiful rooms she had ever seen.

The rooms at Windsor Castle were filled with a clutter of small tables, objets d'art and photographs.

This Drawing-Room contained only the essential amount of furniture and three outstanding pictures.

It was in fact, a picture or poem in itself.

"This is the loveliest room I have ever seen," Avila exclaimed.

"That is what I hoped you would think," the Prince answered. "And it is, as I expected, a frame for you."

"That is the nicest compliment I have ever had," Avila smiled.

"I can think of a number of others," the Prince replied. "As I have supplied you with an English tea I shall be disappointed if you do not enjoy it."

At his suggestion she poured out the tea for them both.

He took it from her but he did not drink it.

Instead he sat down in a nearby chair looking at her in a way which made her feel shy.

"How can you be anything at the moment," the Prince asked, "but Athene, the Goddess of the Household?"

Avila laughed.

"You are well aware," she answered, "Athene had dark hair and, so I suspect, did all the other goddesses. So I do not really fit in."

" 'Athene was the Goddess of all things fair'," the Prince quoted, "and as she, like Apollo, was enveloped with light, I imagine your golden hair would have been quite appropriate for those who wanted to sculpt her."

"I doubt it," Avila said, "and I suppose we shall never know the truth of what exactly they did look like."

The Prince threw up his hands.

"A million or more statues have been made of Athene! But of course in a way you are right. It is only when I can see her living and breathing that I am now aware how beautiful she is."

Avila understood what he was implying.

Somehow, because they were speaking Greek, his compliments were not as embarrassing as they would have been in English.

"You said you had brought me here to see your house," she said quickly. "Now tell me exactly when it was built and who designed it so perfectly that it appears to be a Temple?"

The Prince answered her questions.

Then when they had finished their tea, he took her round the house.

He showed her the many rooms which were exquisitely furnished, and the sunken bath which was still intact.

He said he intended to use it when it was completely restored to its former beauty.

Then when the sun was sinking they went out into the garden.

In the distance Avila could see the deep blue of the sea and the vague outline of several islands.

"You must tell me about the islands," she said.

"That is something I shall be doing tomorrow," the Prince replied.

"It is something you have been saying all day,"

she said, "and I am wondering why tomorrow will be any different from today."

"That is a question I can only answer tomorrow," he replied.

She laughed.

"Now you are being mysterious. I am not sure whether it is a game you are playing to amuse yourself, or whether there really is something mysterious about what we shall do tomorrow."

"I am afraid you will have to wait and see," the Prince answered.

Avila laughed again.

"I suppose it is because we are in Greece. We seem to be talking in a strange manner, as if we were imitating the Sages and all those great men who lived and wrote in Athens."

"How could we do better?" the Prince answered. "As Sophocles said: 'Many marvels there are, but none so marvellous as Man'."

"My Mother has often quoted that to me," Avila said, "but I thought it was extremely unfair and typically male that he did not mention women."

The Prince laughed.

"I think he was well aware that sooner or later women would push themselves to the front and affirm that they were more marvellous than man."

He paused a moment and then went on:

"At the same time Sophocles and every other deep thinker worshipped Athene and the other Goddesses of Olympus."

"It is a strange thing," Avila said, "that ever since I have been in Greece I have realised that it is difficult to have a conversation in which the ancient gods and goddesses are not included."

"I thought you would understand," the Prince said, "that they are included because you are aware, as I am, that they are still here."

Avila looked at him.

"Do you really believe that? Do you think they are on Olympus at this moment, laughing at us?"

"I do not know whether it is Olympus or anywhere else in Greece," the Prince said. "But I am sure as you are, if you will allow yourself to admit it, that the gods and goddesses are still alive, still leading us in their own way to the understanding of life which they possessed."

The way he spoke was very moving and Avila clasped her hands together.

"You make everything I found so difficult sound so simple," she said. "Yet I suppose, when I leave, it will all be difficult again."

"Must you leave?" the Prince asked.

Because it was an unexpected question she turned to look at him.

"I have to go home, as you know, the day after tomorrow," she said, "and I shall not have seen even a quarter of what I want to see."

"I asked you quite simply," the Prince said, "if you must go."

Avila was about to say that she wanted to stay more than she had wanted anything in her whole life.

Then she remembered that she was not just unimportant Avila Grandell, but Her Royal Highness Princess Marigold.

What was more, she was secretly engaged to Prince Holden.

For a moment she could not find words to answer the Prince's question.

When she did not do so he suddenly turned.

"I think it must be nearly time for us to dress for dinner. I have ordered a very special meal for you tonight which I hope you will enjoy. It may be selfish of me, but I have not invited anyone to meet you."

He spoke in rather a hard voice as if he was sweeping away the almost dreamy manner in which they had been talking.

Now they were walking back towards the house, and the shadows from the setting sun were growing longer.

'Perhaps he is hurt because I am not responding to him as I should have done,' Avila thought.

She felt a sudden pain within her heart because in some way she could not explain, he had gone away from her.

When they entered the house he took her to the foot of the stairs.

He did not seem to notice when she looked up at him pleadingly.

"Thank you .. Thank you very .. much for showing .. me .. your .. beautiful .. house and .. garden," she said.

"I am so delighted," the Prince said, "that it pleases Your Royal Highness."

He spoke in what she felt was the conventional way a Statesman would have addressed her.

Then as she started to climb the stairs he walked away.

"What have .. I said? What .. have I .. done?" Avila asked herself.

He had changed suddenly, all in a second.

The caressing manner in which he had spoken to her before had gone.

As she reached her bedroom her maid was not there and she was alone.

She went to the window.

Looking out she could see the sea in the distance as she had seen it from the garden.

The Olive trees were in blossom and the flowers brilliantly beautiful near to the house.

The sun was sinking and yet its rays were still golden.

The sky behind it was turning a soft crimson.

It was all breathtakingly beautiful.

But for the moment all Avila could see was the Prince walking away from her.

"After tomorrow I shall never see him again," she told herself.

Her whole body seemed to cry out with the cruelty of it.

The maid came into the room and suggested that Avila should rest in bed whilst she prepared her bath.

It was brought into the room and when the hot water had been carried upstairs and poured into it, it was scented with the oil of lilies.

Avila thought, as she stepped into it, of the sunken bath downstairs.

One day the Prince would bathe as his ancestors had bathed.

She was sure that when he was doing so he would look like the statues of Apollo that her Mother had shown her.

She had thought from the first moment she saw him that he resembled Apollo.

Princess Marigold had provided her, among the clothes she had brought with her, with some very pretty evening-gowns.

They were of course, black, but they had been made by someone with imagination – the lace was unlined and the tulle transparent.

When she was dressed the gown seemed to her to be rather low in the front.

However it also left her arms and shoulders bare, so she did not mind the rest of it being in black.

It had not struck her until now that Princess Marigold, if she had been here, would have had some jewellery with her.

Because her engagement to Prince Holden was a secret, the Princess had not been wearing a ring when they changed places in the *Traveller's Rest*.

Avila was quite sure that Prince Darius had no idea that Princess Marigold was secretly engaged.

At the same time to make her impersonation more convincing she thought she should wear something round her neck.

As she looked at herself in the mirror she knew that she wanted the Prince to admire her.

She wanted him to go on paying her the compliments which made her shy and at the same time were a music she had never listened to before.

There was a knock on the door and the Greek maid went to answer it.

Avila heard a man-servant saying:

"With His Royal Highness's compliments."

The maid came back to her carrying in her hand some flowers.

Looking at them Avila realised, though it seemed impossible, that the Prince had known what she would want.

What the maid held in her hand was a necklace made of small white flowers.

It was so delicately arranged and the flowers were so small that they might easily have been of precious stones.

Instead they had real petals and tiny leaves.

When she put it round her neck Avila saw it was exactly what she wanted.

It made her look both correctly dressed and really beautiful.

There was a small bunch of the same flowers for the back of her head.

The maid pinned them in place.

When Avila looked in the mirror she knew that she had never looked so lovely before.

Feeling a little self-conscious, but at the same time excited, she went downstairs.

When she went into the Drawing-Room it was to find the Prince there alone.

Slowly because she knew he was watching her, she moved towards him.

It was impossible to look into his eyes until she was actually standing in front of him.

Then because he did not speak she looked at him questioningly.

For a moment there was silence then he said very softly:

"Now I am quite sure that you are Athene."

The caressing tone was back in his voice and Avila felt her heart turn over.

Then he said:

"It is with many apologies that Lady Bedstone regrets that she is so tired that she feels sure that you will understand if she does not join us for dinner."

"I was afraid it was rather a long journey for her," Avila managed to say.

"I am more delighted than I can put into words," the Prince said, "that we can be alone."

Because she felt she should say something Avila replied:

"I am rather surprised that perhaps the British Ambassador and certainly Lord Cardiff did not expect to be your guests."

"As a matter of fact I think that they did expect it," the Prince replied, "but I told them that unfortunately a great number of my relatives were coming to the Funeral."

He saw the expression in Avila's eyes and said quickly:

"I did not lie. I merely said that a great number were coming to the Funeral, and they assumed that they would be staying with me."

"Now you are being very evasive," Avila said. "But how did you know that you wanted us to be alone?"

"I did not know until I met you," the Prince replied. "Then when I saw you, and thought you must have stepped out of my dreams, I knew I wanted to show you my house and talk to you, alone."

"So it all happened on the spur of the moment," Avila said.

"I think it was pre-ordained," the Prince answered. "We were both here perhaps when the house was built first."

Every word he said to Avila seemed to vibrate through her whole body.

She knew she responded not only with her mind, but with her heart and soul:

"He must not know what I feel for him," Avila told herself quickly.

With a tremendous effort she said lightly:

"You are making Greece too difficult for me to understand. Tell me now of your plans for the future. Surely you do not live here alone?"

"I am seldom alone," the Prince answered. "Again it was fate or perhaps a decree of the gods, but I was abroad when my Uncle died and I only returned to Greece three days ago."

He spoke as if in its own way it had been a certain triumph and Avila said:

"And what do you do when you are living here?"

"Look after my Estate. I also play a part in the Government of Greece, and at the moment I am deeply engaged in something which I will show you tomorrow."

Avila held up her hands in protest.

"We are not going back . . tomorrow?" she questioned. "It will be impossible for me to sleep tonight in case I am missing something important from the moment the hands of the clock pass midnight."

The Prince did not dispute her anxiety, but simply said:

"Dinner is ready. May I have the honour, Your Royal Highness, of taking you in to enjoy it?"

He held out his arm as he spoke.

Avila put her hand on it delicately, exactly as her Mother had taught her to do.

They walked down a long cool, beautifully arched passage which led to the Dining Hall.

As they did so Avila thought they might almost be husband and wife on their way to have dinner together in their own home.

It was just a passing thought.

But as it swept through her mind she knew that this was something she would remember and think of when she returned home.

Then there would be no chance of her ever seeing the Prince again.

CHAPTER SIX

Avila woke in the morning with a growing feeling of excitement that today was very important.

She had gone to bed dreaming of the Prince.

She thought as she came downstairs that he looked even more handsome than he had in her dreams.

She had been told when her Maid called her that Lady Bedstone was very sorry but she did not feel well enough to get up this morning.

Avila had gone to see her and found there was really nothing wrong.

The truth was that Lady Bedstone was afraid she might have to walk some distance or perhaps climb up the side of a hill.

"I know what men are like," she said, "when they are showing off something they prize. Quite frankly, Ma'am, I am too old for it."

"I think you are being very sensible," Avila replied, "and I will tell you all about it when I come back."

When she dressed she found among Princess Marigold's black gowns the dress she had worn when she arrived at The *Traveller's Rest*.

It was thin and white.

She put it on, thinking she was unlikely to see anyone except the Prince.

There was a small, simple straw hat to go with it.

She still did not know where they were going.

Because she knew the Prince was expecting her to ask questions, she deliberately did not show any curiosity.

'If he wants to be mysterious,' she told herself, 'then I will let him be up to the last moment.'

They drove only a very short distance to a small bay where she saw there was a yacht moored.

It was quite a small yacht and as the Prince helped her out of the Chaise, having handed the reins to a groom who had sat behind, he said:

"This is the yacht I use when I am visiting the islands. I should have told you before that I have been made a Guardian of several islands, the most important being the one to which we are now going."

"That is, of course, what I am all agog to hear," Avila said.

He was smiling as he said:

"You have contained your curiosity very well, and I promise you that you will not be disappointed."

It was a glorious day with the sun shining and the sea quiet and still.

As soon as they started to move away from the shore Avila stood at the rail looking out over the Aegean Sea.

It was so lovely that she thought perhaps the Prince was just taking her on a tour of the nearby islands.

Then as they moved through what seemed a transparent blue of the sea ahead, the Prince said:

"Have you not guessed where I am taking you?"

"I should be afraid to do that," Avila said. "You have been so mysterious that you would be disappointed to find I have guessed wrong."

"Look ahead!" the Prince said.

She did.

It seemed to her that there were a number of white islands, all shining in the sun and somehow a little ghostly.

"Those are 'The Wheeling Ones'," the Prince said softly. "They seem to wheel round one small island which stands so lonely in their midst."

Avila gave a little start and then she said:

"I know now where we are going."

"I thought you might guess," he answered. "Where else should I take Athene?"

"It is to Delos," Avila said.

Now she felt a strange excitement sweep over her.

She had heard about Delos all her life.

She knew it was where Apollo had been born and to the Greeks the most holy of all their precious islands.

Because it was so exciting she could not think of anything to say.

So they stood in silence until the yacht stopped in a bay where there was a small wooden quay.

It was built high enough for the gangway to be let down on it.

"As I have been coming here so often," the Prince explained, "I found this bay. It saves me from going to the port which is the only place on the island where we would find any people."

He and Avila walked ashore.

Now as they moved inland she could see the low ground which was a mass of flowers.

Anemones in every colour flooded the meadows.

She could see peeping through them just a few gleaming columns and ruins glittering in the sunshine.

It was so lovely that she could only stare at what she was seeing.

It was impossible to put into words what she felt.

The Prince did not move.

Avila had the impression that there was a strange light glittering and shining in the sky and the air itself felt like a dancing, flickering flame.

It was so unusual and so different from anything she had ever experienced.

Without thinking what she was doing she put out her hand and slipped it into the Prince's.

His fingers tightened on hers.

As he did so she felt a mysterious quivering, and could not understand if it was in the air above her or in her breast.

Then as she went on, looking at the beauty of the flowers and the distant little hill, she had for a moment a picture in front of her.

The whole island shone white with Temples.

At the same time she was sure she heard the beating of silver wings, and the whirring of silver wheels.

How long they stood there just holding hands she had no idea.

Then she shut her eyes because it was too intense to bear.

The Prince said quietly:

"The god of Light was born here, and the Greeks are perfectly aware of the strange quality of light which illuminates this island."

"I .. can .. feel .. it," Avila said in a whisper.

"As I knew you would," the Prince answered.

He drew her forward and they started to walk over the anemones.

As he did so he said:

"This is the virgin island and no one was allowed to be born, to die, or to be sick here. As you have just felt, a Divine Light covers it."

"That is .. true. Really .. true!" Avila said in a rapt voice. "When I read about .. Delos I had .. no idea I could feel .. like this, exactly as .. if Apollo was .. still here."

"But he is!" the Prince said firmly. "Every time I come here I become more and more aware that the light of the island still comes from him."

They walked on.

In front of them was a small hill which the Prince told Avila was once covered with Temples.

There were the ruins of them still left peeping out between the anemones, ivy and barley-grass.

Avila could see the ruins of Parian marble, and she had the strange impression that the stones were only waiting to rise again.

As she and the Prince moved amongst them she was aware of the quietness of an unexplained mystery.

They walked for quite some time and then unexpectedly she saw some Olive trees.

Under them stood a table covered with a white cloth on which there were arranged various dishes and plates.

She looked at the Prince for an explanation and he said:

"Here is our luncheon. I thought we would not want to be waited on by servants who might interrupt our thoughts and our feelings. So we will help ourselves."

"How could you think of something so delightful?" Avila asked.

"I was thinking of you," he answered.

They sat down at the table and there were the most delicious things to eat which only the Greeks could make.

There was a golden wine to drink which Avila thought must be the nectar of the gods.

While they ate the Prince told her how in later times many of the lesser gods came to shelter under the wings of Apollo.

"There were temples here to Cybele, Hadad, Astarte and Isis," he said, "and the island became so sacred that few Kings, however avaricious, dared attack it."

"It must have been very, very beautiful," Avila sighed.

"It was so beautiful, with so many treasures on it, that almost every country in the world has managed to steal what was our heritage."

His voice sharpened as he said angrily:

"The Ottoman Turks sent expeditions to the island, and knocked down the statues of the gods to lop off legs, arms and heads. They transported the marble trunks and torsos to Constantinople."

"How could they do .. anything so .. ghastly?" Avila asked.

"All men are greedy," the Prince replied. "But I believe there are still treasures here hidden deep in the ground, which have not yet been found even after two thousand years of pilfering. I intend to find these for Greece and keep them for her."

Avila looked around at the anemones and wondered if there really was anything left of the glory that had been Apollo's.

They had finished their luncheon and the Prince rose and put up his hand.

"Come with me," he said, "and I will show you what I have found."

Avila's eyes lit up.

"Can there really," she asked, "be anything left behind after all these years?"

The Prince did not reply.

He was climbing up the low hill which was just behind where they had eaten.

They had reached some way up when the Prince stopped.

Then as Avila looked to the right she saw what appeared to be a wooden door with a bar across it.

She glanced at the Prince enquiringly and he said:

"Just before I had to go away I discovered a cave which I am sure no one has found before."

He paused a moment and then went on:

"I only had time to look at it briefly, and because I was afraid people might explore it when

I was away I had, as you see, a door placed on the entrance which is locked."

He drew a key from his pocket, opened the padlock and raised the bolt.

He pulled open the door which was roughly made of a heavy wood.

Avila saw inside on the floor there was a lantern.

The Prince picked it up and lit it. Then he said with a smile:

"Now we will go and explore."

She took the hand that he held out to her, and bending their heads because the cave was a low one, they moved forward.

A few seconds later it opened out into a larger cave where the Prince was able to stand upright.

He lifted his lantern so that they could look round.

Avila could not see anything unusual and he said:

"I am sure this cave was used by those who worshipped Apollo. It does not speak of murders or sacrifice but of faith, and to me the promise of Light."

Avila made a little murmur.

It was what she felt too and she was sure that the people who had come here worshipped Apollo with a pure faith.

The cave had an enchantment that she could feel very strongly.

The Prince moved on.

They were just about to enter a further cave when suddenly there was a loud bang behind them.

They both started and turned round.

As they did so Avila was aware that the light that had come from the open door had vanished and there was only darkness.

Even as she was aware of it, she heard the bolt on the door being thrust into place.

A hoarse, ugly voice said:

"Stay in there and rot! You have no right in a cave which belongs to Apollo."

The Prince moved quickly backwards to where they had come.

"You are making a mistake," he said in a commanding voice. 'I am Prince Darius and a Guardian of this island. Open the door that you have just closed!"

He waited and Avila held her breath.

Then suddenly there was a burst of shrill, mad laughter.

"Prince or Beggar," the voice outside jeered, "you have no right here. Only the gods themselves are allowed on this island."

His Greek was coarse and Avila knew that the speaker came from the gutter.

At the same time there was an ominously mad note in his voice and in his laughter.

Now he was laughing again.

"You will rot in the darkness," he shouted. "You will die in agony as other thieves have died and the worms will eat your flesh."

"Now listen to me . ." the Prince began.

Even as he spoke the man outside was laughing again – a shrill, uncanny, unpleasant sound which seemed to rise to a sharp crescendo.

Then it faded slowly.

He was still laughing, and Avila knew that he

was moving down the hill up which they had climbed.

Then he must have hurried over the anemones until they could no longer hear him.

The Prince set down the lantern he was holding in his hand and put his shoulder to the door.

Although he pushed against it with all his strength it did not move or even creak.

Suddenly Avila was frightened. Very frightened!

Without thinking of what she was doing she threw herself against the Prince, clinging to him as she asked:

"Shall .. we .. really .. stay here .. and die?"

He put his arms around her and without speaking bent his head and his lips were on hers.

He kissed her possessively and fiercely.

For a second she stiffened and then the wonder of it swept over her and she felt her body melt into his.

He kissed her for a long time.

She felt as if it was a part of the mystery, wonder and beauty of the island.

Once again she could hear the beating of the silver wings and the whirring of silver wheels.

It was only when the ecstasy of it was so wonderful that she felt she could no longer be alive, that the Prince raised his head.

"My Darling, my Sweet," he said. "I have waited so long for this. Now I know that you are mine, as you were meant to be a million years ago."

Avila was looking up at him and by the light of the lantern he could see the rapture in her eyes.

"I love you," he said softly. "Now tell me what you feel about me."

"I .. love .. you," Avila said a little incoherently and hid her face against his shoulder.

The Prince held her very close.

"I swore a long time ago," he said, "that I would never marry anyone until I found someone like Athene, who would feel as I feel when I come to Delos, that Apollo is here in the light, as he had been ever since he was born."

He felt Avila quiver against him and he went on:

"I knew when I first saw you that you were what I had been seeking all my life and thought I would never find. Yet I had to make quite sure I was not mistaken."

He drew in his breath before he continued:

"When we came here today and I saw and felt what you were feeling, I knew I had found the mystic love all men seek and few are lucky enough to find."

He put his fingers under Avila's chin and turned her face up to his.

"We shall be very happy together, my Darling. How could we be anything else when Apollo has blessed us and we are both of us, part of him and of Athene."

He kissed Avila again before he said:

"And now, my Precious, we must find our way out of this mess."

Because he had made her forget anything but his kisses, Avila awoke to reality with a start.

They were locked in a cave and no one might ever find them.

The Prince read her thoughts.

"Sooner or later my people will come to look for us," he said. "But it would be more dignified and certainly more pleasant if we could find our own way out of this prison."

He released Avila as he spoke and picked up the lantern.

He walked back to where they had been when the door had shut behind them.

They had just been stepping into a third cave.

As the Prince went ahead holding the lamp high, Avila could see that the ceiling here was higher than in the other caves.

But she thought depressingly that it was merely because the hill was rising outside.

It would not be possible to dig through it when they did not have a spade or anything to use but their own hands.

The Prince was looking round.

At the far end of the cave there was what looked like a great pile of earth that might have covered an Altar.

It rose up halfway between the floor and the ceiling.

"I think," he said after a moment's inspection, "it would be wiser to try to break our way out through the sides of the door."

Avila did not answer.

She was in fact praying to the God to whom she had always prayed, and also to Apollo.

"Save us! Save us!" she murmured in her heart. "It may be difficult, or perhaps impossible, for anyone to find us, and we will be cold here at night and we will also be hungry."

It all swept through her mind.

At the same time she knew what her Father would say and she herself believed, that their only hope would come from a Power greater than mankind.

The Prince had already stepped back into the second cave and she ceased praying and looked up.

Then she was aware, now that he had taken the lantern with him, that there was a faint chink of light in the ceiling at the far end of the third cave.

She gave a cry of excitement and the Prince turned round.

"What is it, my Darling?" he asked.

"Look at that! Look! I was praying and when I opened my eyes I could see light."

The Prince came back into the big cave and saw where she was pointing.

There was, he could see, a very faint glimmer of light against the darkness.

He took off his coat and put it down on the ground beside the lantern.

Then he climbed up onto the mound of earth at the far end of the cave.

Some of it crumbled as he did so.

Then as he stood working at the roof above his head, he made a small hole and more light came in.

He began pulling frantically to make the hole larger and still larger until the sun shone on his head and on his face.

Even as he did so Avila gave another cry.

The earth on which he was standing and which covered what she had thought might have been an altar, was crumbling away.

As it did so it revealed something white and shiny.

Because she was so excited Avila ran forward.

She knelt down and brushed the soil from what the Prince's weight had revealed.

Even as the Prince stepped down to join her, she realised she was looking at an exquisitely carved statue.

It was cracked and one arm was missing, but it was impossible not to recognise that it was a statue of Apollo.

The Prince knelt and put his arm round her.

"He has come to us when we most need him," he said. "I am very grateful, my Darling. But even more grateful because he has given me you."

Then he was kissing her again.

Kissing her with wild, passionate kisses which were not only an expression of love.

They also expressed his relief that the fear of what might have happened had dissolved.

. . . .

Very much later that afternoon they were moving over the still blue sea towards the mainland.

Avila was thinking that they had passed through the most amazing and unusual experience and had been saved by the god of Delos himself.

It was the Greeks' belief that the island was under a spell.

They too had been spellbound as they managed to climb up out of the cave, then opened the door and collected the statue of Apollo to take back with them.

The Prince had carried it to the yacht.

When he had placed it safely in the Saloon he had put his arms around Avila to say:

"It will stand on the most beautiful Altar which has ever been built for Apollo, and bless us so that we will never lose the happiness we have at this moment and which will be ours for eternity."

It was only as she felt the yacht move into the open sea that Avila had come back to reality.

The wonder of Delos, the thrill of being kissed by the Prince and knowing that he loved her had made her completely and absolutely forget.

Now she remembered he had proposed to the Princess Marigold and not to Avila Grandell, the daughter of a country Vicar.

She could hardly realise herself that she was not the Athene the Prince believed her to be or the wife chosen for him by Apollo.

As the mainland came in sight the sun was sinking, and the crimson in the sky was reflected on the waves.

For a moment it seemed to Avila that it was like her own blood, bleeding from the heart that must lose everything that mattered in life.

"You must be tired, my lovely little goddess," the Prince was saying. "But I have to take you back to Athens because I promised the Ambassador you would be there tonight so that you could leave early in the morning."

"How . . early?" Avila asked in a voice which did not seem like her own.

"I think about midday, or perhaps an hour earlier," the Prince answered. "But I promise I will be with you much earlier. We have to make

116

plans about how soon I shall follow you to England. I suppose you will have to ask permission of Queen Victoria to marry me."

Avila did not answer.

The agony of what he was saying was almost unbearable.

"You are tired," he said gently. "We will talk about it tomorrow, and of course when I have followed you to England."

He paused for a moment before he went on:

"I think it would be a mistake for me to travel with you. Her Majesty might think that I am presuming on her hospitality. I know she is reputed to be very difficult, but I cannot believe she will not accept me as your husband."

As they drove back in the Chaise to Athens after disembarking, Avila said very little.

She was only acutely aware of the Prince being beside her and her love for him welling up like a tidal wave.

It was impossible to think of anything but how handsome he was and how she would love him despairingly to the end of her life.

"There will never, never," she told herself, "be another man like him."

They were late arriving at the British Embassy and by this time it was nearly dark.

It had taken them a long time to get out of the cave.

When they returned to the yacht they had to walk slowly because the statue of Apollo was so heavy.

The British Ambassador greeted them enthusiastically.

"I have been worrying about Your Royal Highness," he said to Avila. "If you had not arrived soon I would have had to send out a search party."

Avila thought how this had very nearly been a necessity.

"I must apologise for being late," the Prince said. "But I will leave the Princess to tell you of the very exciting discovery we have made."

"Nobody would be surprised at anything that happens on Delos," the British Ambassador answered.

Avila held out her hand to the Prince.

"Thank you so much for a very .. wonderful day," she said. "It .. is .. something .. I will .. never .. forget."

He took her hand and kissed it.

Just for a moment they looked into each other's eyes and it was impossible to look away.

Then without speaking the Prince turned towards his Chaise.

"I have put back dinner half-an-hour, Your Royal Highness," the Ambassador was saying, "so you do not have to hurry unduly."

"Thank you," Avila managed to answer.

She had been told before they left that there was a party tonight.

She was glad in a way that the Prince was not staying.

It would have been difficult, in fact agonising, to have to talk to anyone else when he was there.

Avila thought when he had walked away from her, that it was the last time she would ever see him.

That exactly was what he had to do.

She was halfway up the staircase when she stopped.

"I think, Your Excellency," she said to the Ambassador who was still in the Hall, "we should arrange to leave early in the morning. Perhaps no later than nine o'clock. I know that Lord Cardiff is very anxious to get back to England as soon as possible."

"He is indeed, Ma'am," the Ambassador replied. "I know he will be very grateful for your thoughtfulness."

"Then you will arrange it?" the Princess said.

"Of course," the Ambassador promised. "I will give orders that you will leave here at eight-thirty."

Avila went on up to her room.

As she did so she knew that darkness encompassed her.

She could no longer feel or see the light of Apollo.

CHAPTER SEVEN

Avila stood on deck watching until Athens was out of sight.

She knew she was saying goodbye, not only to Greece, but also to a love which she would never find again.

At last, when she could only vaguely see the coastline, she went below.

Her maid had already unpacked and her cabin was empty.

Taking off her hat and her jacket, she sat down on the bed.

She was trying to think clearly, and not to heed the agony that was in her heart.

'I love .. him. I love .. him!' she kept thinking.

She felt again the wonder of his kisses and the rapture he had given her yesterday from the moment they had stepped onto Delos.

As the Battleship steamed on the sea grew rougher.

One of the storms which appear suddenly in the Mediterranean made it pitch and roll.

Avila was not upset by the sea.

In fact, it was a relief to think that now she had

an excuse not to go and sit in the cabin with the Greek Ambassador and Lord Cardiff.

They would expect her to be sea-sick and, like Lady Bedstone, take to her bed.

All she really wanted was to be alone.

To think over what had happened and remember every word the Prince had said to her.

Gradually the agitation she had felt in getting away from the British Embassy before he arrived, subsided.

She began to think more sensibly about the future.

If he followed her, as he intended to do, he would find on arrival in England that Princess Marigold was engaged to Prince Holden.

The question then was whether he would go straight back to Greece, or whether he would visit Windsor Castle.

Avila knew it was extremely important that he should not go to Windsor.

If he asked questions there, the Queen might suspect what had actually happened.

Avila wondered what she could do to prevent there being any possibility of this.

It was then she remembered, with a sense of relief that Prince Holden would be meeting her when she arrived at Tilbury.

Her Mother would also be waiting, as they had arranged, at the *Traveller's Rest*.

She would go back to the country with her, never to be heard of again.

"I am grateful, of course, I am grateful for having seen some of Greece," she told herself. "But I know I will never feel the same again, and there will be emptiness in the future that can never be filled."

That night when she went to bed, the ship was still pitching and rolling.

However all she could think of was the Prince, and she cried herself to sleep.

It was something she was to do every night of the voyage.

Because it was so rough in the Bay of Biscay she was able to stay in her cabin without it causing any comment.

Lady Bedstone sent her messages to which she replied but otherwise she was alone with her thoughts and her memories.

As they drew nearer to England, Avila knew she must make an effort to join the Ambassador and Lord Cardiff.

The coast was actually in sight when, dressed in the black gown she had worn when she came on board, she joined the two gentlemen for luncheon.

They appeared to be delighted to see her.

"We have been very worried about you, Ma'am," Lord Cardiff said. "The Captain says he had never known the sea so rough, but as you know, this can happen in the Spring."

He paused a moment and then continued:

"I have congratulated the Captain on not having lost time, despite the weather."

Avila sat down with them and tried to eat a sensible meal.

While she was in her cabin she had had no wish to eat anything.

She only pecked at the food which her Greek maid conscientiously brought her.

Now she told herself she had to return to ordinary life and behave in an ordinary way.

"I have been telling Lord Cardiff," the Greek Ambassador was saying, "how much I enjoyed the visit to my own country, even though it was for the sombre occasion of a Funeral."

"I know Your Royal Highness enjoyed it too," Lord Cardiff said, "and I am sure what His Royal Highness Prince Darius showed you of the Greek islands was interesting."

"Very . . interesting," Avila managed to say.

"I consider him just the right person to be the Guardian of some of the islands," the Greek Ambassador remarked. "He has always been extremely knowledgeable about our history, and I am quite certain if there are any treasures left in Delos, or the other islands, he will find them."

Lord Cardiff laughed.

"I think you are being optimistic. The islands have been stripped in every century, and the French have been busy in this."

"That is true," the Greek Ambassador remarked, "and I am furious at hearing what they have taken from Delphi."

"I do not blame you," Lord Cardiff said. "At the same time, because the statues of Greece are so perfect, they must belong to the world."

The two men then began a somewhat heated argument as to whether the treasures from one country should be taken to another.

The Greek Ambassador made a special point of claiming that the Elgin Marbles should be returned to where they belonged.

Avila stopped listening to them.

She was thinking of the beauty of the statue they had found in the cave.

She wondered if there were any more under the pile of earth on which Prince Darius had stood.

If there were she knew she would never see them.

Again she felt the agony of loss, almost as if the statues were her own children.

It was in the early afternoon that they finally reached Tilbury.

As they did so Lord Cardiff made Avila a flattering speech.

He told her how much he had enjoyed her company and how splendidly he thought she had carried out her duties.

"I shall tell Her Majesty she could not have sent anyone who would have represented Great Britain better," he said.

"Thank you," Avila answered.

"That is certainly true," the Ambassador said, "and you will not forget, Ma'am that I shall be asking you to honour our Embassy with a visit. I will keep you notified of all the entertainments that take place there."

"I shall look forward to hearing from you," Avila said.

As *H.M.S. Heroic* moved slowly into dock, she went on deck.

She could not remember what time Prince Holden was expecting her.

She wondered what she should do, if by any chance he was late.

Lord Cardiff and the Ambassador would expect

her to be carried away immediately to Windsor Castle.

She need not have worried.

When she looked down at the Quay she could see the Prince with the Harbour Master waiting for her.

There were a number of carriages which were to take the different members of the party aboard the Battleship to where they wished to go.

Prince Holden came aboard.

He greeted the Captain, then the Greek Ambassador and Lord Cardiff.

The latter quickly made his farewells and hurried down the gangway to the carriage which was waiting to take him back to Whitehall.

Once again he congratulated Avila on the success of her visit to Greece.

He repeated that he knew Queen Victoria would be delighted with the report he intended to give her.

When he had gone, the Greek Ambassador made no move to follow him.

Prince Holden, who had already greeted Avila effusively, said to her:

"I think now we should be leaving."

"Yes, of course," she answered.

She shook hands with the Captain and the other Officers and thanked them for a pleasant voyage.

The Captain responded by saying what a privilege it had been to have her aboard.

Avila was escorted down the gangway by Prince Holden.

The Greek Ambassador was following them.

Avila got into the chaise and the Prince deliberately waited until the Greek Ambassador went ahead.

Avila knew he would undoubtedly think it rather strange if, having come straight from the ship, he saw them stop at the *Traveller's Rest*.

Finally, as his carriage disappeared out of sight they started to drive slowly along the Quay.

Lady Bedstone was in a closed carriage behind them.

Although she might think it odd for them to stop at the Hotel, she would, Avila knew, not make any fuss about it.

As soon as the Prince had driven the Chaise a short distance from the ship, he asked:

"Was everything all right?"

"Everything!" Avila replied.

"No one was suspicious that you were not the Princess?"

"No, not at all, and Lord Cardiff was very complimentary, as you heard just now."

"I cannot tell you how grateful I am to you," Prince Holden said. "But of course, we must be very careful that no one has the slightest suspicion of what has occurred."

"No one in Athens queried for a moment that I was not .. who I was .. supposed to .. be," Avila assured him.

Try as she would, she could not help there being just the suspicion of a sob in her voice.

She hoped however, that the Prince would not notice.

"You have obviously been absolutely splendid!" he was saying. "I know that Her Royal Highness has a special present for you with which to express

126

her gratitude and I thought, as you live in the country, you might like me to give you a horse."

"A horse?" Avila exclaimed. "Of course I would, and it is very, very kind of you, but there is no need for you to give me anything."

"There is every need," the Prince replied. "You have given me happiness, and that is something that cannot be bought over the counter."

Avila laughed.

"That is true, and I have been fortunate enough to see Greece."

She wanted to add:

". . and *un*fortunate enough to lose my heart!"

But that was something nobody must ever know.

The Prince drew up his horses outside the *Traveller's Rest*.

"You will find your Mother in the same bedroom which you used before you left," he said, "and thank you from the bottom of my heart for being so brave."

Avila managed to smile at him.

Then she stepped out of the Chaise and hurried into the Hotel.

She pulled the veil over her face and knew the Proprietor, who was waiting to escort her to the stairs, could not see her clearly.

It was not likely, she thought, that he would notice any difference.

Except she knew she was very different from the carefree girl who had left the *Traveller's Rest*.

She had started out then on what she had thought would be an exciting adventure.

It had been that, and so much more, and she knew now that she would never be the same again.

In a way, she had grown up.

She was no longer a girl, but a woman.

As a woman she had learnt the wonder and the glory of love and, inevitably, the agony and despair of losing it.

The same maid in a mob-cap guided her up the stairs.

"There be a lidy waitin' for Yer Royal Highness," she said.

She knocked on a bedroom door, opened it and bobbed a curtsy as Avila went inside.

She saw her Mother standing by the dressing-table.

She ran towards her and was aware that Princess Marigold was more or less concealed on the other side of the bed.

"Avila, dearest! You are all right?" Mrs. Grandell asked.

"Yes, perfectly, Mama," Avila replied.

She threw back her veil so that she could kiss her Mother.

Then turning to the Princess she curtsied.

"Everything went off perfectly, Your Royal Highness!"

"I am extremely grateful to you," Princess Marigold replied.

She was wearing a white Summer dress, not unlike the one Avila had worn when she had arrived at the Hotel from the country.

Now she started to change into a black gown which she had brought with her.

It was unpacked and lying on the bed.

"I shall need my bonnet," she said. "I am sure you found the veil useful in case people stared at you too closely."

"Yes, indeed," Avila replied, "and thank you, very much, Ma'am, for the lovely gowns you put in the trunk. I am sure His Royal Highness will arrange to have it collected from my home."

She thought he would do that when he sent her the horse he had promised her.

"Oh, do not worry about them," Princess Marigold answered. "If they are of any use to you, do keep them! I hate black and I have enough of it to last for a thousand Funerals!"

Mrs. Grandell laughed.

"I am sure, Your Royal Highness, you have been told over and over again that black is very becoming to your fair hair. But thank you for your generosity to my daughter."

"I shall always be very deeply in her debt," Princess Marigold said, "and although we are unlikely to see each other again, I shall always remember how you helped me at a time when I most needed it."

Mrs. Grandell was doing up the back of her gown as she spoke.

Avila had taken from her head the bonnet with its dark veil and laid it on the bed.

Princess Marigold sat down at the dressing-table to put it on.

As she did so she said:

"I know you will be interested to hear that tomorrow my engagement to Prince Holden is being officially announced, and we are actually being married in two weeks' time."

"Then of course I wish Your Royal Highness every happiness," Mrs. Grandell said.

"I expect Her Majesty is furious that everything is being done in such haste," Princess Marigold went on lightly, "but I am so afraid that somebody else may die, and we are plunged into mourning again, that we are taking no chances!"

"I think that is very wise of you, Ma'am," Mrs. Grandell said, "and of course you have Avila's and my good wishes."

"I shall be very happy," Princess Marigold said firmly. "Although Her Majesty may not approve, I am quite content to have what must be a small wedding before I leave for my husband's country."

"You will be married, I imagine, at Windsor Castle?" Mrs. Grandell said.

"I am afraid so," Princess Marigold replied, "and my Bridesmaids will have to hurry to have their gowns made as I shall have to hurry to buy my trousseau."

She was speaking as if the whole thing was rather a joke, which Avila found surprising.

She rose from the dressing-table saying:

"Thank you again, Avila. You have not yet told me if Greece is as beautiful as you expected it to be."

"It was very, very wonderful, Ma'am," Avila said in a low voice.

"Then we have both had very satisfactory holidays," the Princess smiled.

She put out her hand to Mrs. Grandell.

"Thank you for all your help," she said. "I hope one day your daughter will be as happy as I am."

She smiled at them both, and as they curtsied she went towards the door.

When she reached it she pulled the veil over her face, then slipped out.

Avila knew that Prince Holden would be waiting for her at the bottom of the stairs.

No one would suspect for a moment that she was not the same person who had just walked up to them.

"Now you must change your gown," Mrs. Grandell said to Avila. "Then we can go home."

Her daughter turned round so that her mother could undo the buttons at the back.

As she did so Mrs. Grandell said:

"I have missed you, Dearest. Tell me what you thought of Greece."

"It was . . even more . . wonderful than I expected it . . to be."

"I want to hear everything, from the moment you left me here," Mrs. Grandell said, "and of course what places you visited in Athens."

For a moment Avila thought it would be impossible for her to speak of what she had seen and felt when she had been with Prince Darius.

She could remember all too vividly the compliments he had paid her as she gazed at the marble maidens supporting the portico of the Erechtheion.

She could remember what he had said the next day when he compared her to Athene, and asked her to be his wife.

It was easy while her Mother was helping her change, to say little.

It was more difficult when they were driving

back home in the closed Chaise which the Prince had hired for them.

Only by pretending that she was tired and shutting her eyes as if she wanted to sleep did Avila manage to say very little.

She did however, describe the Funeral and the Reception at the British Embassy.

"I am disappointed that you could not stay in the Palace," Mrs. Grandell said. "It is very beautiful inside and some of the statues it contains are breathtaking."

"I did not know you had been in the Palace, Mama!" Avila said in surprise.

"I did not mention it because I thought it was unlikely that you would ever have a chance of seeing it," Mrs. Grandell said quickly. "Tell me about the Parthenon."

Avila stammered a few sentences.

Then as she remembered the Prince's voice and the nearness of him, she shut her eyes.

The cross-examination was agonising.

She could only pray that her Mother would never guess how she was suffering.

Her Father was waiting to greet her when she got home.

"I hope you have enjoyed your holiday," he said. "Your Mother has been worrying about you all the time you were away, but I cannot think why!"

"It was all very exciting, Papa," Avila said, "and it was interesting to see places which Mama has told me about. I know you will be pleased to hear that everyone thought my Greek was very good."

"How can it be anything else, when you have a

Greek Mother?" the Vicar asked. "Now, thank goodness, you are back. Your Mother has been behaving as if you had disappeared to another Planet, and we would never see you again!"

Avila managed to laugh.

"I am back," she said, "and now it will . . all seem like a . . dream."

That was the truest thing, she thought, she had ever said.

Of course it was a dream; a dream so beautiful and so perfect, that it could never come true.

When she was alone all she could see was the anemones covering the ground in front of her.

All she could feel was the Prince's hand holding hers.

She was vitally aware of the strange light.

It was different from the light in any place she had been to before.

She wondered if she would ever know again the mysterious quivering, the beating of silver wings, the whirring of silver wheels.

They belonged to Delos, and she would never see Delos again or the Prince!

Then the wonder of those moments would gradually fade away until she doubted to herself if she had ever really been aware of them.

"How can I bear it? How can I go on living?" she asked that night.

She threw open the window and looked out at the stars overhead.

They were the same stars that had twinkled above her when she was in Greece.

Now they seemed far away and some of their enchantment had gone.

How was it possible that she had been transported to know the ecstasy of the gods?

And now to be thrown into the dark emptiness of being human?

Suddenly Avila felt the tears running down her cheeks.

"I have . . lost . . him! I . . have lost . . him!" she sobbed.

She knew she had lost not only the Prince but somehow Apollo.

She had also lost, or perhaps left behind, her soul.

Having cried herself to sleep, she woke in the morning feeling that everything was an effort.

She just wanted to stay where she was, and not have to speak to anyone.

Then she told herself that it would be a great mistake for her Father or Mother to think that her visit to Greece had not been just a normal holiday.

Having acted the part, she must go on acting, now as herself.

She dressed and went downstairs before anyone else was up.

Leaving the house, she walked to the stables.

She could not help hoping Prince Holden would remember to send her the horse he had promised.

It was then she recalled somewhat belatedly that the Princess had given her a present just before she left the bedroom.

Because her Mother was in a hurry to leave Avila had not opened it at the time.

She had put it into her handbag, and never gave it another thought.

It was upstairs in a drawer where she always kept her bag and her gloves.

The horses seemed glad to see her and nuzzled against her.

She told herself that when she had had breakfast she would go riding.

That at least she would be able to do alone.

She had always had permission to ride in the Park which belonged to the Duke of Ilchester.

It occurred to her that she had never seen the Prince on horseback.

She knew however from the way he drove that he would be an outstanding rider.

His horses would instinctively respond to anything he asked of them.

"How can he be so different from any other man?"

She knew the answer.

He had told her what it was when he said that they had known each other for a million years already.

For the first time she wondered if he would feel incomplete without her.

Then she was sure it was too much to ask.

He might seem like a God, but he was also a Man of the World.

He travelled; he had an important position in his own country and great possessions.

Moreover he thought it was Princess Marigold who had visited Athens for Prince Eumenus's Funeral.

The Greek newspapers would be sure to carry the story of her engagement and later, of her marriage.

When he read that, the Prince would know it was impossible for him, as he had wanted, to marry Princess Marigold.

He would doubtless be hurt and offended that she had not told him of her engagement.

The result would be, Avila reasoned, that he would not come to London as he had intended.

He would remain in his own country and doubtless, in time, would find another woman he would take to Delos.

She too would seem to him like Athene.

Avila wanted to cry out because it hurt her to think of it.

And yet she knew she was being sensible and that was exactly what would happen.

The sooner she accepted the inevitable, the better.

She left the stable and walked in the garden.

It seemed to her very small.

Although the flowers were brilliant in the sun they could not compare with the masses of anemones which covered Delos.

"It is over! It is over! It is over!"

She forced herself to repeat the words until she was sure they would go on repeating themselves in her subconscious mind, even when she was asleep.

It had been a glorious interlude.

Now she knew that the Prince would not even think of her as a woman he had loved.

She had kept from him the knowledge that she was engaged to be married to another man.

He would think she had been deceitful, that she had lied.

That was something she knew he could never forgive.

Now the pain in Avila's heart was even worse than it had been before.

There was nothing she could do – nothing!

She heard her Mother calling her, which meant that breakfast was ready.

As she walked back to the house she was saying over and over again in her mind and her heart:

"It is over! It is over! It is over!"

. . . .

The next two days passed slowly, so slowly that it seemed to Avila as if each hour was a century of time.

"I do not know what is the matter with you!" the Vicar said to his daughter. "You seem to me to have had such an exhausting holiday that you need another in which to recuperate!"

"I am . . only a little . . tired, Papa," Avila said.

Her Mother was going to visit someone at the end of the village who was sick.

When she had driven away Avila went back into the garden.

She knew she had to make an effort, and not loaf about as she had been doing for the last two days.

She walked past the yew hedges and under the trees to where there was a small stream.

Her Mother always referred to it as the 'Water Garden'.

It was very attractive, but for the moment Avila could see only the blue mist over the Aegean Sea.

She could hear the soft waves lapping against the shore on the Island of Delos.

She had forced herself not to cry for the last two nights.

Now her unhappiness could no longer be controlled and she felt the tears come into her eyes.

Then to her surprise she heard footsteps coming towards her.

She supposed that her Father needed her, and turned round.

Then she was spellbound.

She thought she must be dreaming.

It was not her Father who was approaching, but Prince Darius.

For a moment when he reached her, they could only stand looking at each other.

Then he held out his arms.

Without speaking, without even thinking, Avila flew towards him.

He pulled her close to him and his lips came down on hers.

She felt once again as if the whole world was enveloped in a vivid light.

She heard the silver wheels moving overhead.

Prince Darius kissed her not gently, but possessively until, as had happened in Delos, her body melted into his.

A long time later he raised his head to say:

"How could you leave me? How could you go away without a word? Why did you not tell me the truth?"

It was impossible for Avila to speak.

She could only stare at him, the tears still wet on her cheeks.

Gently he kissed them away.

Then he said:

"Now tell me you love me!"

"Y . you . . know that I . . love you," Avila said. "B . but . . why are you . . here? How did you know . . where to . . f . find me?"

"I knew," he answered, "when you left without telling me you were going that I had to follow you. I boarded the very next ship, but I arrived in England too late to go to Windsor Castle that night."

Avila gave a gasp of horror.

"Y . you . . have not . . been to . . Windsor Castle?"

The Prince smiled.

"Does that frighten you, my Darling? Not half as much as it frightened me, when I found a strange young woman impersonating you."

Avila was trembling.

"You . . you spoke to . . Princess Marigold?"

"When she heard that her visitor had come from Greece, she was sensible enough to receive me alone," the Prince replied, "and the moment I saw her, I knew she was an imposter."

Despite herself, Avila could not help giving a little choked laugh.

"You cannot . . have accused . . the Princess of . . impersonating me! But . . did you not think she was me?"

"Do you suppose for a moment I did not know that while there was a resemblance, there was something vital missing which you and I found together in Delos?"

Avila knew exactly what he meant, but she was

still frightened about what further had happened at Windsor.

"Was the Princess .. very .. angry that .. you were .. not deceived .. as everyone .. else .. had been?" she stammered.

"No, and she understood that I had to know the truth, the whole truth, otherwise I might go to the Queen."

"Y . you .. would not have .. done that?" Avila cried.

"I would have turned the whole world upside-down to find you!" the Prince declared. "If it meant accusing Queen Victoria of fraud, I would not have hesitated to do so!"

"Princess Marigold .. must have been .. very .. frightened .. of .. you!" Avila gasped.

"She was frightened, but intelligent enough to understand that what I wanted was you. So she told me where to find you."

He did not wait for Avila to reply, but kissed her again.

He kissed her until she felt as if she was being carried up into the sky and she was in the sun.

Only when they could breathe again did the Prince say:

"And now, my Precious, we are going to be married as quickly as possible so that I can take you back to Greece with me."

"B . but .. you cannot .. marry me!"

"Why not?" he demanded.

"Because you thought you were .. proposing to someone who is .. Royal .. like yourself .. and I am .. just very .. ordinary."

The Prince laughed and it was a very happy sound.

"How can you be ordinary," he asked, "if you are Athene, and given to me by Apollo himself? Come – let us go and talk to your Father who I was told is writing his Sermon and could not be disturbed."

Avila gave a little laugh.

"So the servants . . told you to come into . . the garden to . . find me?"

"They said Miss Avila was in the garden, and I knew that was the little goddess for whom I was looking."

"Y . you are not . . angry because I . . deceived you?" Avila asked nervously.

"Very angry that you did not trust me," he answered, "but now I understand it was something you could not do. I was even more angry to think you could believe you could go away and forget me."

"I would . . never have . . forgotten . . you," Avila replied, "and I have been so . . desperately unhappy since I . . left Athens."

He looked down at her.

"You are thinner, and there are lines under your beautiful eyes," he said. "So, Heart of my Heart, I believe you."

"I swear I will . . never . . never lie to you . . again," Avila said, "but this was not . . my lie, and incidentally . . Papa does not . . know why I went . . to Athens. He just . . thinks I was . . invited by Princess Marigold to go with her and help her to brush up her Greek on the voyage."

The Prince did not speak and she added quickly:

"Please .. please .. do not .. upset him!"

"Do you think I would do anything that would upset you?" the Prince asked. "Now let us go and find your Father and tell him we wish to be married."

They walked towards the house.

As she had done before, Avila slipped her hand into his.

She knew as a thrill ran through her when his fingers closed over hers, that once again they were one.

It was the same feeling she had had when they were on Delos. Earlier, in fact, when he had taken her to the Parthenon.

They entered the house and as they did so Avila was aware that her Mother had returned.

She was in the Drawing-Room and the door was open.

"Come and meet my Mother," Avila suggested.

"That is something I am very anxious to do," Prince Darius answered.

They walked in and Mrs. Grandell, who was standing by the window, turned round in surprise.

"Mama," Avila said, "this is .. His Royal Highness Prince Darius .. of Kanidos whom I .. met when .. I was .. in Greece."

She rather stumbled over the introduction.

Then she was aware that the Prince was staring at her Mother in a strange way.

Mrs. Grandell moved towards him and Avila was aware of a worried expression in her Mother's eyes.

As she reached the Prince he exclaimed:

"But – surely I am not mistaken? You are Cousin Lycia!"

"And you – are Darius!" Mrs. Grandell said. "I think I would have recognised you although you are older and much bigger than when I last saw you."

Avila looked from one to the other.

"Are you . . saying that . . you know Mama?" she asked the Prince.

"Your Mother is my Cousin," Prince Darius explained, "and Princess Lycia was, when she was your age, one of the most beautiful girls in the whole of Greece."

Avila stared in astonishment.

"*Princess* Lycia?" she questioned.

"I have never told Avila what happened," Mrs. Grandell explained quickly.

"I think you would like to know," the Prince said, "that I saw your brother a month or so ago and he said that he often wondered what had happened to you. And now that your Father is dead, he intends coming to England to try to find you."

"My brother said that!" Mrs. Grandell exclaimed.

"I think your whole family feels the same," Prince Darius replied, "just as my family believed you had been very harshly treated."

"What are you . . talking about . . what are you . . saying? You must . . tell me!" Avila cried.

The Prince smiled and took her hand in his.

"Your Mother ran away with the man she loved," he said, "just as I am prepared, my Darling, to run away with you, if your Father and

Mother will not accept me as a suitable husband for you."

"And . . Mama ran away . . and she is really a . . Princess?"

"A very important Princess," Prince Darius replied. "Her Father was Prince Alexius of Zacynthos, one of our largest islands. But he was an exceedingly proud man and was horrified when his breathtakingly beautiful daughter wanted to marry a not very important Englishman."

"My husband may not have a title," Avila's Mother interrupted, "but his family is one of the oldest Saxon families in existence and held office in the County of Devonshire long before the arrival of William the Conqueror."

The Prince laughed.

"I am only putting it from your Father's point of view," he said, "for he expected you, as you were so beautiful, to marry no less than a King."

Avila's Mother laughed too.

"But I fell in love," she said, "with a young man who had just come down from Oxford, and was touring Europe."

"So you . . ran away with . . Papa!" Avila said excitedly.

"We ran away and my Father cursed me for disobeying him. He declared I was no longer one of his family and he would not acknowledge me as his daughter."

There was a note in her voice which told Avila how it had hurt her.

"He also stripped me of my title and everything I possessed," her Mother went on. "But I was completely content, my Dearest, just to be your Father's wife and your Mother."

"No one can understand that better than I can," the Prince said, "for I would marry Avila, as you call her, if she were the daughter of a Fisherman. But you will understand it will make things far easier for me, and for her, when it is known that her Mother is Princess Lycia and a Cousin of my Mother whom everybody loved."

"I loved her too," Avila's Mother said.

"Your other relatives and there are quite a number of them," Prince Darius said, "still love you and will welcome you home. I promise you, that is the truth."

He smiled before he added:

"Now I know why my lovely Avila and Princess Marigold resemble each other."

"Why?" Avila asked.

"The Princess's Father, Prince Dimitri of Pana-eros," he answered, "was the nephew of your Mother's Mother."

Avila laughed.

"So I am actually related to Princess Marigold?"

"Yes, you are second cousins and your grand-mothers were sisters," the Prince agreed, "but it would be wise not to mention it at the moment, at any rate, not until we arrive in Greece."

He saw the question she wanted to ask before it reached her lips.

"I would like to marry Avila in Athens," he said to her Mother, "and if you agree, we will go there immediately, because I cannot wait to make her mine. We have also some very important work to do in Delos."

"Married .. in Greece!" Avila exclaimed. "I cannot imagine .. anything more .. wonderful!"

"That is what it will be," the Prince said quietly.

"I must go and tell your Father," Avila's Mother said.

She ran from the room and the Prince drew Avila to him.

"How could we have imagined," he asked, "that our Fairy Story could have such a happy ending?"

"I could not .. think it was .. possible," Avila said.

"With Apollo and Athene looking after us," the Prince replied, "everything is possible. That is why, my Lovely One, we will be married in Athens, and our honeymoon will be spent in the islands, the most exciting being Delos where we will discover together what else is hidden in the third cave."

CHAPTER EIGHT

Prince Darius did not tell Avila what he felt when he went to the Embassy as arranged, to find she had already gone.

At first he could not believe it possible and said firmly:

"I think you must be mistaken. I understood Her Royal Highness was leaving later this morning."

"Her Royal Highness left the Embassy at 8.30," was the reply, "and I understand the *H.M.S. Heroic* sailed at 9 o'clock."

If anyone had given him a body-blow the Prince could not have been more stunned.

He had gone to bed thinking he had never been so happy.

He had found the one woman in his life who was the wife for whom he had sought.

Princess Marigold he believed was completely and absolutely the other half of himself.

He had always been quite certain that the Greek Legend was true.

The Creator, they said, had divided the human beings He had created because he was lonely.

One half of Him was soft, sweet, beautiful and

spiritual, the other was strong, protective and far-seeing.

Prince Darius had set in his heart a shrine which contained the ideal woman he would marry.

She would help him with his work in Greece and his protection and interest in the Islands especially Delos.

Even when he was a small boy Prince Darius wanted to be a Guardian of that particular Island.

Now it was his, he felt as if he had been given the most priceless jewel the world had ever known.

When he had taken Avila there he was almost certain he was right in thinking she felt as he did.

That the air was alive and the gods were speaking to them as they had spoken to Apollo.

He had not been mistaken.

He had known that his long search was at an end.

He had found the true love which all men sought and only some were fortunate enough to find.

Yet incredibly she had left Athens without telling him.

Without apparently even leaving a note behind to explain her strange behaviour.

He thought it was beneath his dignity to ask but he had to know the truth.

"Did Her Royal Highness leave a message for me?" he enquired.

The man to whom he was speaking shook his head.

"There was no message Your Royal Highness," he replied.

It was then Prince Darius knew that he had to find out why Marigold had left.

Could she have really changed her mind at the last moment and no longer cared for him?

It seemed so impossible that he almost laughed at the idea.

He had never been in love before.

Naturally there had been many women in his life.

Because he was so handsome and of such importance they had pursued him ever since he had grown up.

He would not have been human if he had not accepted what had been offered to him so freely.

He knew quite well that almost every woman with whom he came in contact, looked upon him as Apollo.

Yet there was a difference between them and Avila.

He confessed quite simply to himself there had always been an expression in their eyes which he knew was an invitation.

In fact, now he thought it out, he was aware of the truth.

Whilst the other women he met looked upon him as Apollo the man, Avila looked upon him as Apollo the God.

That he told himself, was the difference he wanted.

The difference he sought and the difference he thought he had found.

It was typical of his quickness of mind that he decided to follow Princess Marigold and learn what had happened from her own lips.

He sent a servant post haste back to his house to collect his luggage.

He himself went to the docks to find what was the next ship leaving for England.

He was informed that a large liner was leaving that evening at 6 o'clock.

He booked himself the most comfortable cabin available and waited for his servant to join him in Athens.

In the meantime so that no one should be suspicious or interested in his movements, he went back to the Embassy to see the Ambassador.

He appeared very much at his ease.

He explained to the Ambassador that he had misunderstood the time the English Party was leaving.

It was important that he should have wished Her Royal Highness, 'Bon Voyage'.

It was then he learnt it was she who had changed the time of departure.

It was entirely her suggestion the *H.M.S. Heroic* had left so early.

This only confused the Prince more than he was already.

When finally he boarded the liner he was bewildered in a way he had never been before.

There had been one woman that he had very nearly married who had been Greek.

Her family was as important as his own.

Everyone had told him how suitable she was to be his wife.

His relations had almost begged him on their knees to marry her.

It was, they pointed out to him, extremely important he should have an heir.

Also it was usual for those of the old and revered families to marry young.

Because they were so persuasive he actually considered this particular choice of theirs more seriously than he had any of the other young women who had been brought to his notice.

She was certainly lovely, and her figure was perfect.

Her face had been admired by every artist in the country.

"If I have to marry," the Prince said to himself, "why not her?"

Finally because she was very much in love with him he was on the point of saying the four words that would seal his fate.

Then he thought he would take her to Delos.

Delos meant so much to him.

He liked going there alone and disliked his friends either criticising or worse still, bemoaning the Temples that had been lost or plundered.

They would chatter on until he could not bear to hear the same sentences again and again.

To take the woman he was to marry to Delos would he thought be the final test.

If she felt as he did the strange air that came from the gods then he would certainly marry her.

He would know he was doing the right thing.

They had gone to the island one evening when the sun was sinking.

To the Prince the air was alive with the mysticism he could not put into words.

Yet he knew it was there for those who felt as he did and were in touch with the gods.

She looked round appearing even more beautiful as the light from the sky haloed her head.

The stars seemed to shine in her eyes.

Then she said in a slightly artificial voice:

"What a pity this place is in such a mess and everything that was worthwhile has been stolen."

The Prince was taking her back to the mainland.

Once again he vowed he would never marry anyone until they felt as he felt in Delos.

All the way when he was travelling towards England he was thinking of how Princess Marigold had quivered against him when he kissed her.

How she had known there was a strange light glittering and shining in the sky.

Also the air itself felt like a dancing, flickering flame.

It was what the Prince had felt and he could read her thoughts.

He knew what she was feeling by looking into her eyes.

Then she put out her hand and slipped it into his.

As his fingers tightened on hers, he had known she felt a mysterious quivering between them and he felt the same.

He was sure that she had heard as he did, the beating of silver wings and the whirring of silver wheels.

He remembered how he himself had said quietly:

"The God of Light was born here and the

Greeks were perfectly aware of the strange quality of light which illuminates this Island."

"I can . . feel . . it," Avila said in a whisper.

How could she have invented anything like that?

How could she have been anything but absolutely and completely truthful.

Her feelings were his feelings and nothing would ever persuade him that was not the truth.

All through the turbulent Bay of Biscay and the long run up the Channel he was turning over and over in his mind exactly what had occurred.

He was reliving the moment in the cavern when she had flung herself against him as she asked:

"Shall we . . really have . . to stay . . here and . . die?"

He had known at that moment she was his.

When he bent his head and found her lips he knew it was something that had been ordained since the beginning of time.

He had found what he had always been seeking.

He kissed her for a long time and felt her body melt into his.

Only when they were both a little breathless did he speak to her.

He saw by the light of the lantern the rapture in her eyes.

No woman could have looked more beautiful and at the same time spiritual.

No woman that he had ever known had looked at him as if he was Apollo the God in whose territory they were standing.

Then the question was back again as to why if she felt like that, had she left him?

He arrived at Windsor Castle the following morning.

He was so early that the more elder Aide-de-Camp was not on duty.

It was therefore a young man who had taken his demand to speak with Her Royal Highness Princess Marigold straight to her private apartment.

Princess Marigold had finished breakfast but had not yet sent for Colonel Bassett to cope with her correspondence.

When the Aide-de-Camp had said His Royal Highness Prince Darius of Kanidos desired to see her, she had stiffened.

It was a shock because she had never anticipated that anyone from Greece would follow Avila home to England.

If the Prince was talkative he might wittingly or unwittingly cause a great deal of trouble.

She had therefore thought quickly and said to the Aide-de-Camp:

"I will see Prince Darius at once and alone. Do not inform my Ladies-in-Waiting that anyone is with me."

"Very good, Ma'am," the Aide-de-Camp said.

While he was fetching the Prince, the Princess moved around rather restlessly.

She was not certain how to compete with anyone who made trouble.

She was wishing desperately that Prince Holden was with her.

He would be coming to the Castle later in the morning but that was of no help at this moment.

The door opened.

"His Royal Highness Prince Darius of Kanidos, Ma'am," the Aide-de-Camp announced.

Princess Marigold was standing at the window.

For a moment because she was frightened she did not turn round.

Then as the Prince did not speak she slowly looked towards him.

Just for a moment she saw an expression on his face which told her what he was expecting.

Then it changed abruptly.

He walked towards her saying:

"I am afraid Ma'am, I have been taken to the wrong room. I asked to see Her Royal Highness Princess Marigold."

"I am Princess Marigold," she replied nervously.

"Not the Princess Marigold who came to Athens for the funeral of my uncle?"

"You are quite certain of that," Princess Marigold asked.

"Completely and absolutely," Prince Darius replied. "Although I admit there is a slight resemblance."

Princess Marigold looked towards the door as if she felt someone might be listening.

Then she said:

"Please help me and whatever happens you must not say that here."

"Say what?" Prince Darius asked.

"That I am . . not the Princess you . . met in Athens."

"Then where is she?" the Prince asked.

Now there was a note in his voice which told the Princess he was determined to hear the truth.

"I want your help," she said. "Please be very careful what you say."

He sat down and Princess Marigold started at the beginning.

She told him how angry she was when she was told she had to go to Greece because she knew Queen Victoria was trying to prevent her from marrying the man she loved.

She knew as she explained what she felt for Prince Holden that Prince Darius was sympathetic.

By the time she finished her story he understood exactly why she had behaved as she had.

He thought it amazingly clever on her part that no one had the slightest idea that she had been with Prince Holden when she should have been in Athens.

"If you told the Queen," Princess Marigold said, "she would be very, very angry. So please understand and go away as quickly as you can."

"I will leave immediately," Prince Darius replied. "If you will tell me where I can find the person who impersonated you so cleverly."

Princess Marigold hesitated.

"Why do you want to see her?" she asked.

"Because I am going to marry her," the Prince said, "and quite frankly nothing and no one will stop me."

The Princess laughed.

It was a very happy sound.

"What could be better," she said, "and you will take Avila away to Greece and no one will ever guess for a moment that I have a double somewhere in England."

156

"Just tell me where I can find her," Prince Darius insisted, "and I promise Your Royal Highness neither of us will ever trouble you again, unless of course you wish to come to visit us."

"I might well do that one day," the Princess smiled, "but promise me you will not talk to anyone in the Castle before you leave."

"You can trust me," Prince Darius said. "I swear that everything you have told me will be shared only with my future wife."

The Princess went to her writing desk and wrote down Avila's address.

Then as she gave it to the Prince she said:

"You are quite right to fight for what you want, that is what I had to do and I have won. But I do not want any repercussions or reproaches."

"Of course not," Prince Darius agreed, "and may I wish Your Royal Highness every happiness in the future."

"And I wish you the same," Princess Marigold said, "and I think if we both get our own way, we are very lucky people."

"And very persistent ones," Prince Darius smiled.

He left her and hurried to find even faster horses to carry him to the country and to Avila.

When the first excitement of his arrival and his insistence they should be married immediately had subsided slightly, Avila said:

"We must be very careful that we do not betray Princess Marigold. As I expect you realise Queen Victoria would be very angry if she knew what had happened."

"I have given the Princess my word," Prince

Darius said, "that I would not speak of it to anyone but you, my Darling."

"But supposing when I go back to Athens as myself, people will think it very strange that I look like Princess Marigold."

"Greek families," the Prince said, "are so closely related to each other over the years, that it is not surprising that quite a number of Greeks resemble each other."

He paused for a moment and then he said:

"Looking as you do at the moment, my Precious, without that heavy black, you might be several years younger than the Princess."

"I suppose that is a compliment," Avila said. "If I was several years younger I would be back in the school-room and you might find me very dull."

"I would never do that," the Prince said. "To me you are everything that I have ever wanted and I will love you whatever age you are, even when your hair is white."

Avila laughed.

"Then I suppose because you are like Apollo you will never grow old," she said, "but always remain the same, a God of Light and Healing, driving across the sky. It is not fair."

The Prince had laughed and pulled her into his arms.

"You are so beautiful, my Precious, as your beauty comes from inside rather than out, it will increase and be even more blinding to mere mortals, as the years pass."

"I hope that is true," Avila said. "Please love me, whatever I am like."

"You can be quite sure of that," he answered.

He then started once again to make arrangements for her Father and Mother to come to Athens as quickly as possible.

"Avila has to have a trousseau," Mrs. Grandell said, "and that will take time."

"Time is what I cannot allow you," the Prince said. "I want Avila with me as speedily as possible. I am going to go ahead merely so that I can arrange that everything is perfect for you. At the same time I am a very impatient bridegroom."

Both the Vicar and Mrs. Grandell realised this was the truth.

Then Mrs. Grandell said a little tentatively:

"My husband will have to ask permission of the Duke of Ilchester to be away, as he is the Duke's Private Chaplain."

She hesitated for a moment and then added:

"Actually the Duke and Duchess are the only people who knew who I was and where I came from. When my husband was fortunate enough to be offered this position as the Duke's Chaplain and the Vicar of the village, he of course, made enquiries as to whom he had married."

Prince Darius smiled.

"I expect he was surprised."

"I rather thought he might be shocked that I had run away from my family. But as you understand, I was in love."

"Just in the same way as I am in love with your daughter," the Prince said. "I will speak to the Duke and I am sure everything will be arranged to suit you both."

They took him to the Duke's house.

The Duke was delighted to meet Prince Darius,

having met some years ago other members of his family.

When he heard he was to marry Avila he congratulated him saying:

"She is not only lovely but ever since a child, she has been one of the sweetest young girls my wife and I have ever known."

"You will understand," Prince Darius said, "I want to be married as quickly as possible and not to have to hang about, miserable because we shall seem almost at the other ends of the world from each other."

The Duke replied:

"I do understand and of course, Grandell can stay with you as long as you want him. I presume you wish him to marry you?"

There was a little pause before Prince Darius said:

"That is what I hope to arrange, but I think the Vicar will understand that it will have to be a double wedding."

He thought that Avila's Father might expostulate, instead he said:

"Of course it would make things very much easier if you could arrange that, because I want, above all things, to marry my own daughter."

"Of course," Prince Darius agreed.

Finally after what seemed to Avila endless conversations, everything seemed to be arranged.

They had two perfectly happy days riding the Duke's horses.

She wanted to show the Prince the countryside she had lived in ever since she had been born.

She loved the way he appreciated everywhere they went and the country people they met.

She knew that every moment they were together she loved him more than she had the moment before.

She knew too that he felt the same.

They had only to look into each other's eyes to talk without words.

When he kissed her she knew the wonder and glory she had felt in Delos was still with them.

At last the Prince said everything had been arranged and he must return home.

The night before he left he took Avila into the garden after dinner.

It was still not dark although the first evening stars were coming out in the sky.

"Promise me," he said, "that you will think about me every moment that I am away."

"I shall be counting every second until I can be with you again," Avila answered.

"I am afraid to leave you," the Prince said putting his arms around her. "I could not go through the agony I felt all the way here when I thought I had lost you and you no longer loved me."

"How could you think that?" Avila said. "I cried every night when I was alone because I thought I would never love anyone again and I would be unhappy all my life."

"That is something that will never happen," Prince Darius said. "I love you my Precious and I swear I will make you very happy."

He pulled her against him and kissed her until she felt she was a part of him and they could not be any closer.

Then he took her back into the Vicarage.

She went up to bed knowing that she would dream he was still kissing her.

He left next morning.

Only when the Chaise that was carrying him to London was out of sight did Mrs. Grandell say firmly:

"Now we have a great deal to do and unless you are going to make your future husband very angry we shall have to hurry."

It was certainly a hurry to find the clothes she wanted.

To buy the gowns she felt Prince Darius would admire.

Fortunately there was an excellent seamstress in the village who could alter the gowns they brought from London.

Therefore they could buy things that were already made.

Only Avila's wedding dress took a little longer than anything else.

This was because Prince Darius had told her Mother exactly what he wanted.

"It seemed a strange thing for the bridegroom to choose the bride's gown," Mrs. Grandell said.

"Because I am Greek I understand what he wants," Avila said. "I am sure he wishes me to look like one of the goddesses."

"Not one of them but Athene," Mrs. Grandell replied, "and that is as you know, aiming very high."

"We must not disappoint him," Avila said nervously.

"I am quite sure you will not do that," her Mother answered.

Finally they set off from Tilbury in the liner that was on its way to India.

Avila could hardly believe that she was leaving England.

After this she thought I shall be living in Greece and my husband will be Greek and so will my children.

She was aware as she had never been before that her Mother was very Greek.

She knew as they approached the Mediterranean that Mrs. Grandell was worrying how her family she had left so many years ago would receive her.

She had run away knowing that nothing mattered except her love.

She could honestly say she had never regretted doing so.

At the same time she had sometimes felt very lonely for her family.

She had longed to see her sisters and brothers and of course the friends with whom she had been brought up and their families.

She could hardly believe that fate had moved in such a mysterious manner to take Avila back to Greece.

She had to admit however, that Prince Darius was the most charming young man.

Only as the ship moved into port did Mrs. Grandell stand rather close to her husband.

It was as if she was afraid of what might be waiting for her personally.

The first person to come aboard was Prince Darius.

Avila was waiting for him and as soon as he stepped on deck she ran towards him.

He kissed her despite the presence of the Captain and other Officers.

She said in a rapt little voice that only he could hear:

"You have . . come! It seems like a . . million years until I . . saw you . . again."

"Ten million for me, my Darling," he answered.

Then behind him was a tall, good-looking man about 40 years of age.

He ignored Avila and went straight to her Mother.

"Welcome home, Lycia," he said and kissed her.

Avila saw the tears come into her Mother's eyes as she said:

"Oh! Ptolemy, it is wonderful to see you."

"And to see you back where you belong," her brother said. "I think you should know that your title has been restored officially this morning and you are now Princess Lycia as you have always been to us."

Mrs. Grandell wiped away her tears.

It was Avila knew, a moment of overwhelming happiness that her family accepted her again.

She saw her Uncle was shaking hands with her Father and she looked up at the Prince.

"Now everything is all right," she said.

"Of course it is," the Prince answered, "because you are here and I am never going to lose you again."

It was something that he made very sure of the following day.

He had arranged for them to stay at the British Embassy.

Avila was very touched when she learned that she and the Prince were to be married early in the British Embassy Church.

There was to be no one to witness the Ceremony except her Mother and the British Ambassador.

"You will understand, my Darling," the Prince said, "that all my family and all my friends who have known me since I was a child wish to come to the Cathedral."

He kissed her forehead before he went on:

"We will be married according to the Greek Orthodox faith in which we will bring up our children."

Avila blushed and looked a little shy and he said:

"We have to do everything together and where we worship outwardly is of course, important to the outside world."

The way he spoke told her without him saying any more what he was thinking.

She and he together would also worship the Gods which were so very near to them.

Yet officially they must pay tribute to the faith in which they had been brought up.

"You . . think of . . everything," she said softly.

His fingers tightened over hers as he said:

"I think of you and nothing else is of any consequence."

When Avila put on the beautiful Wedding

Gown that had been made at the Prince's request, she knew that it was a perfect garment for the part she had to play.

It was in very soft chiffon which was not popular amongst brides at the moment.

It clung to her figure and made her seem almost ethereal and part of the sunshine.

The skirt swept out at the back and made a train of its own.

Over the softness of the gown was a lace veil made by Greek fingers at least two centuries earlier.

She expected the Prince to lend her some of the superlative jewels which her Mother had told her were famous in Greece.

The wreath which came with the veil was of small white lilies and field flowers which she knew grew in Delos.

There was a bouquet of the same blossoms.

When she entered the Embassy Church to find Prince Darius waiting for her he thought she might have stepped straight down from Olympus.

Her Father married them and Avila was certain it was a service they would both remember.

Every word he spoke told them he understood what they were feeling for each other.

Also that the God he worshipped and in which he believed was blessing them.

When they rose after the blessing the Prince lifted back Avila's veil.

He kissed her very gently on the lips.

It was a kiss not of passion but of dedication.

She knew he vowed himself to protect and love her for the rest of his life.

A little while later Avila drove to the Cathedral with her Father.

Prince Darius had gone ahead.

Because everyone in Athens had heard about the ceremony which was to take place the roads were lined with people who waved and children who threw flowers.

To Avila it was very exciting.

When she stepped out at the Cathedral the crowds cheered and wished her luck as she walked up the steps.

The huge Church was filled with both the Prince's and her Mother's relations.

Everyone who knew either of them wanted to be present on this particular occasion.

Every pew was packed.

There was a full choir and the service was taken by three priests.

To Avila it was a little awe-inspiring.

The Prince was beside her and made certain she made no mistakes.

When they walked down the aisle those watching thought no two people could look more radiantly happy.

Outside the Cathedral the crowd had increased since they had gone inside.

There were cheers as they reached the open carriage in which they were to travel to the Palace.

Having heard of the marriage King George had sent a message to say he was deeply disappointed he could not be present on such an occasion.

But he placed his Palace at their disposal for the Wedding Reception.

It was a kind action which endeared him to the people he was just getting to know.

It was, Avila thought later, a very intelligent thing to have done.

The Palace was very impressive.

The flowers which the Prince had arranged to have everywhere made the air fragrant.

There was a huge Reception first to which everyone who had been in the Church was invited.

Then there was a 'Wedding Breakfast' for the families and relatives.

These amounted to over 100 and naturally there were speeches from some of the older members.

Besides a very amusing and witty reply by Prince Darius.

There was a room in the Palace for Avila to change from her Wedding Gown into a going-away dress.

It was particularly attractive with a little hat which was not much larger than the wreath she had worn at the Wedding.

She looked lovely yet at the same time very young.

When she said 'Goodbye' to her Mother the Princess Lycia was once again nearly in tears.

"Enjoy yourself my Darling," she said. "I know Darius will take care of you."

"You can be quite certain of that," the Prince said.

They drove away amid cheers and a cloud of rose petals.

As they went down the street he said:

"Now we can have the wedding the way I want."

"Another wedding!" Avila exclaimed in surprise.

"You have been marvellous," he said. "You have said all the right things to the right people and now my Precious one, we will be alone. There is so much I want to tell you and so much that matters only to you and me."

She did not understand but she was so happy she just pressed her cheek against his arm.

He was driving an open Chaise in which he had taken her driving before.

The horses were even faster and she thought even more impressive.

They did not talk very much as they left the City and the houses behind.

Avila was just happy to be with him.

Then to her surprise instead of going as she had expected to his beautiful house, she saw they were nearing the sea!

A short while later she was aware that his yacht was waiting for them.

She wanted to ask questions but felt it was a mistake.

When they went aboard the Captain congratulated them and then put out to sea.

The Prince did not take her below as she had thought he would.

They stood on deck and watched until the Islands came in sight.

They seemed to glitter as the sun was sinking in the East.

Suddenly Avila realised they were going to Delos.

She did not say what she had discovered aloud, but the Prince said:

"That is where I thought we should both be and in case you are frightened, my Precious one, let me tell you that I have arranged for us both to be very safe even though you will not see who is guarding us."

For a moment Avila was afraid the man who had shut them up in the cave might spoil the happiness of their night together.

Then she knew the Prince would have seen to everything.

They drew nearer and nearer.

Then they stopped in a different part of the Island to where they had been previously.

There was a small bay with a wooden jetty jutting out on one side.

Avila found they could step on to it from the yacht.

The Prince took her by the hand and they walked off the jetty and up a path on to the top of the cliff.

It was then she saw they were in a part of the Island where there were trees.

The ground was covered with anemones that had been there before; the scent was in the air.

They walked in the shade along what seemed an easy path until suddenly to her surprise, she saw a building.

She was not certain what it was.

But it was something she had not expected to find on Delos.

Then as she drew nearer she saw it was made

with trees and the branches still had the leaves on them.

The Prince did not speak.

Then when they reached the strange building he pulled aside a green curtain.

It blended in with the trunks which constituted the walls.

Inside there was a room.

At one end there was a large bed draped with soft muslin curtains.

To her surprise she saw on the other side there was no wall.

She could see there was a large pool on which the last glimmering light of the sinking sun was shining.

She looked at the Prince in surprise and he said:

"I built this for you, my Darling. I knew that tonight of all nights, we should be in Delos where the gods will be near us and will bless us for all the years that lie ahead."

"How .. could .. you .. think .. of .. anything so .. wonderful?" Avila exclaimed.

She could see now that there was a soft carpet on the floor.

There were small pieces of furniture that seemed to melt into the background of the tree trunks.

The Prince drew her into his arms.

"We will talk about it later, now I want you close to me."

He kissed her very gently.

Then he disappeared behind the bed where Avila thought there must be another room.

She knew what he wanted.

Quickly she slipped off her pretty going-away dress and put it down on a chair.

She then saw lying on the bed a diaphanous nightgown.

It must have come from her trousseau earlier in the day.

She slipped into bed and now her heart was beating and she felt a wild excitement creeping up over her.

From the moment they had set foot on Delos she had felt again the strange quivers hanging in the air that had been there before.

Outside on the pool the sun had gone.

Now she thought there was a reflection from the stars up above.

Then the Prince came in.

She heard him but because she was shy, she could not look at him but continued to stare at the water.

Instead of coming to her as she expected, he began to pull at a rope she had not noticed hanging beside the bed.

With a rustle the ceiling overhead moved slowly back until it almost reached the muslin curtains which fell on either side of the bed.

Now she could see the stars above in the sky.

She gave a gasp and stared up at them.

Then the Prince was beside her pulling her into his arms.

"Now we have the stars in the sky and the wonder and glory of Delos for our wedding night," he said.

"How .. could .. you .. think .. of .. anything so .. wonderful, so .. perfect," she asked.

"That is what it will be my Precious," he answered, "my little goddess, my wife."

He was kissing her. Her eyes, her cheeks, and the softness of her neck.

Avila knew there was a vivid light shining into the room and the air around them was like a dancing, flickering flame.

She could feel her whole body quivering against the Prince.

As he kissed her and went on kissing her she could hear the beating of silver wings and the whirring of silver wheels.

"I love . . you, I love . . you," she wanted to say.

But her heart said it to his heart and her soul to his soul.

Then as Darius made her his the gods blessed them with the dazzling light of Apollo.

Other Books by Barbara Cartland

Other Novels, over 500, the most recently published being:

A Coronation of Love
Royal Lovers
Royal Eccentrics
A Duel of Jewels
The Duke is Trapped
The Wonderful Dream
Love and a Cheetah
Drena and the Duke
A Dog, A Horse and A Heart
Never Lose Love

Spirit of Love
The Eyes of Love
The Duke's Dilemma
Saved by a Saint
Beyond the Stars
The Innocent Imposter
The Incomparable
The Dare-Devil Duke
A Royal Rebuke
Love Runs In

The Dream and the Glory (In aid of the St. John Ambulance Brigade)

Autobiographical and Biographical:

The Isthmus Years 1919–1939
The Years of Opportunity 1939–1945
I Search for Rainbows 1945–1976
We Danced All Night 1919–1929
Ronald Cartland (With a foreword by Sir Winston Churchill)
Polly – My Wonderful Mother
I Seek the Miraculous

Historical:

Bewitching Women
The Outrageous Queen (The Story of Queen Christina of Sweden)
The Scandalous Life of King Carol
The Private Life of Charles II
The Private Life of Elizabeth, Empress of Austria
Josephine, Empress of France
Diane de Poitiers
Metternich – The Passionate Diplomat
A Year of Royal Days
Royal Jewels
Royal Eccentrics
Royal Lovers

Sociology:

You in the Home
The Fascinating Forties
Marriage for Moderns
Be Vivid, Be Vital
Love, Life and Sex
Vitamins for Vitality
Husbands and Wives
Men are Wonderful

Etiquette
The Many Facets of Love
Sex and the Teenager
The Book of Charm
Living Together
The Youth Secret
The Magic of Honey
The Book of Beauty and Health

Keep Young and Beautiful by Barbara Cartland and Elinor Glyn
Etiquette for Love and Romance
Barbara Cartland's Book of Health

General:

Barbara Cartland's Book of Useless Information with a Foreword
by the Earl Mountbatten of Burma.
   (In aid of the United World Colleges)
Love and Lovers (Picture Book)
The Light of Love (Prayer Book)
Barbara Cartland's Scrapbook
(In aid of the Royal Photographic Museum)
Romantic Royal Marriages
Barbara Cartland's Book of Celebrities
Getting Older, Growing Younger

Verse:

Lines on Life and Love

Music:

An Album of Love Songs sung with the Royal Philharmonic
Orchestra

Films:

A Hazard of Hearts
The Lady and the Highwayman
A Ghost in Monte Carlo
A Duel of Hearts

Cartoons:

Barbara Cartland Romances (Book of Cartoons)
has recently been published in the U.S.A., Great Britain,
and other parts of the world.

Children:

A Children's Pop-Up Book: "Princess to the Rescue"

Videos:

A Hazard of Hearts
The Lady and the Highwayman
A Ghost in Monte Carlo
A Duel of Hearts

Cookery:

Barbara Cartland's Health Food Cookery Book
Food for Love
Magic of Honey Cookbook
Recipes for Lovers
The Romance of Food

Editor of:

"The Common Problem" by Ronald Cartland (with a preface by the
Rt. Hon. the Earl of Selborne, P.C.)
Barbara Cartland's Library of Love
Library of Ancient Wisdom
"Written with Love" Passionate love letters selected by Barbara
Cartland

Drama:

Blood Money
French Dressing

Philosophy:

Touch the Stars

Radio Operetta:

The Rose and the Violet
(Music by Mark Lubbock) Performed in 1942.

Radio Plays:

The Caged Bird: An episode in the life of Elizabeth Empress of
Austria. Performed in 1957.